HEAR OUR HANDS

By Elaine Jamyson

1

The dedication of this work goes to Mamamease. We talked many times about me writing a book and you always told me I could. I can't wait to see you again.

Special thanks to my husband, the artist, Tasha for being you, and all those who support me in my writing.

PROLOGUE

The first thing Jess was aware of was the incessant beeping. She wished it would stop. But she could not pinpoint where it came from. Why not? And why couldn't she feel anything?

Slowly, awareness settled over her and she realized she was in the hospital.

The events of the previous night came flooding into her mind. She remembered showing up for a job that turned into a gang initiation. She did remember that much. She was acutely conscious each time another member violently raped her. The faces were not clear in her memory, but each male had a distinctive odor. She would never forget how they smelled.

Suddenly, an ache began to set in and almost every bone in her body was screaming with pain. Just at that moment, the nurse came in, pushed a few buttons on the monitor and Jess drifted back off into oblivion.

Chapter One

The mountain air was a welcome change from city pollution. Jessica Turner, owner/operator of "Hear Our Hands", a sign language interpreting agency, took a deep breath of that crisp clean air and slowly exhaled. Being that she had never taken a liking to coffee, she was enjoying a huge mug of hot chocolate.

She had escaped to the mountains a month earlier. As soon as the hospital released her after the attack, she packed her bags and fled to her grandfather's mountain home with her mother.

She kept reminding herself that her officemates, Dylan and Sophia, were more than competent enough to handle the business while she was away. But she knew that she would eventually have to return to work.

As Jess was enjoying her hot chocolate on the porch, she noticed a car coming up the dirt road in the distance. She immediately tensed up. No one knew she was hidden away here. But before she was about to succumb to a full-blown panic attack, she recognized the car as an unmarked police car.

Jessica vaguely remembered Lieutenant Tory Trent who visited her in the hospital. He was very gentle when interviewing her about the incident. Most of the time, she was very curt and sometimes downright rude. Yet, the officer maintained a calm, composed demeanor and would leave her alone.

It was her mother who insisted that she give Lt. Trent the cabin information. Now it appears as though he shared that information with someone else. How did she know the gang members didn't have connections within the police department?

As her anger bubbled up, it quickly subsided. The police representative who stepped out of the car was Tory Trent himself.

"Good morning, Ms. Turner. How are you coping today?"

Jess remained silent. She recalled a conversation in the hospital where she reprimanded him for asking how she was doing. She suddenly felt embarrassed. He remembered something that small.

As he walked up to the porch, she studied him. She never was clear-minded enough at the hospital to get a good look. He was about 6'3" and 315 pounds of muscle. His skin was the color of caramel. When he walked, he had an air of confidence as well as authority. His curly hair was cut low to his head; two deep dimples creased his cheeks as he smiled gently at her.

She couldn't help but contrast her own looks with the lieutenant's. Men always found her attractive, but she did not kid herself into thinking that she was glamorously so. She had been blessed with rich, chocolate skin and deep, captivating, brown eyes.

She was slightly jealous of his dimples; she only had one on the right side of her face. She blinked as Trent started speaking to her.

"You have not been answering my calls. I took it upon myself to come and check on you. I hope I haven't startled you."

It was at this point that Jess realized she was staring. She was mesmerized by his light brown eyes and could not concentrate on what he was saying.

"Forgive me. Please have a seat. May I get you something to drink?"

"No thanks. This is a brief visit. I wanted to fill you in on the investigation so far and see if you have remembered anymore details. But you have not answered my questions. How are you coping?"

"Not very well. I know I need to go back to work and be with my friends, but I just keep putting it off. I keep saying 'maybe tomorrow'."

"It's understandable that you are feeling that way. I am not here to rush you. I do wish to set up an appointment with you when you return to civilization. It would be helpful to get as many details as possible concerning the events that happened that night. The things that happened to you are terrible, and I wish to apprehend these guys as soon as possible."

"I know, I know," Jess sighed as she got up to pace the porch. "I have to face reality eventually. Today is Wednesday. Why don't we say Friday at 11 o'clock? I will come to the precinct."

"That will be fine, Ms. Turner." Trent flashed a beautiful smile that seemed to light up the entire porch. "I will be waiting." He waved and strolled back to his car.

As Jess watched him walk back to his car, she began to feel guilty about not talking to him right then. She had been remembering several small details that she could have shared with him. But she didn't want to invade her serene surroundings with such ugly nightmares.

****

On the ride back home from the mountains, Jess decided that she wanted to drive. She didn't want to sleep, which is what she did on the way up. She wanted to plan. Throwing herself back into her work seemed like a great idea.

She called her office and was greeted with an ecstatic staff.

"Jess, it is so good to hear from you!" gushed Sophia.

"We were sooo worried about you!" Dylan chimed in.

She was obviously on speaker. "Hi guys. I apologize for not answering your calls. But I did get all your messages. You guys are great. Thank you. How are things going at the office?"

"Good thing you called. There is a school calling and the parents of the deaf student are requesting you to be the interpreter. Do you feel you are ready to go back to work? This will be a difficult assignment because the school houses emotionally and behaviorally disturbed children."

"I will do it. It is time for me to jump back into the saddle. Email me the specifics." Jess was eager to have a change of pace. "I will be in the office tomorrow morning."

She didn't want to tell them she had to go to the police station and relive the events that plague her dreams. She began to wonder how much her officemates knew about what happened to her.

She decided not to dwell on the subject as she rolled down the windows, turned up Ledisi on the radio and sang her way back home to Atlanta.

Chapter Two

Jess had always been keenly affected by her sense of smell. Her family used to tease her about it as she was growing up until one day, she sniffed out a gas leak. That was the same day the gas hot water heater had exploded in their home. Because of her nose, the family had evacuated just in time. Even though she continued to be the brunt of jokes concerning her sense of smell, her family respects her when she talks about scents. However, none of her family was with her now. She heard the doubt in the voices of the sketch artist.

"Lady, I can't sketch smells," was his response when she told him she only remembered their scents.

Tory Trent had not been there when she arrived at the precinct at 10:45 a.m. As a sign language interpreter, she was in the habit of arriving at her assignments at least

15 minutes early. She was informed that he was out on a call.

Jess selfishly and silently cursed him. How could he not be there when he promised that he would be waiting for her?

The officers there did not keep her waiting. They immediately set her up with the sketch artist. Later, they gave her a stack of paperwork to fill out.

"I am not about to do this," Jess thought to herself. "I am not ready. What difference would it make?"

She jumped up from her seat, threw the paperwork in the nearest trash can, spun around and almost knocked over Tory Trent.

"I'm sorry to have kept you waiting. I hope they got you started on the . . ." His voice trailed off as he noticed the discarded documents.

"Would you like a cold Coke? I have some in my office. We could go in there and talk for a minute." As he spoke, he calmly turned and walked toward his office.

Jess hesitated. More than anything she wanted to run and distance herself from the memories. Yet, another part of her wanted to be heard. She wanted to prove that she was not crazy.

Trent's office was small and extremely tidy. The color scheme was chrome and black and the chrome was shining in the sunlight that came through the solitary window. There were no dressings on the window, which added to the tidiness of the room.

The gray and black leather chairs in front of his desk were simple and very comfortable.

"Please have a seat," invited Trent as he opened a small refrigerator door located underneath his desk. He handed Jessica an 8 oz. bottle of Coke.

"I'm trying to cut back on my caffeine intake. So, I buy these little bottles."

He opened his coke, lifted it to his mouth and appeared to drink it down in a matter of seconds.

"The sketch artist was informing me about your sense of smell. Talk to me about what you smelled that night." Trent figured he would just jump into the topic.

Jess closed her eyes and surprisingly felt comfortable enough to speak.

"One thing I remember smelling was a mixture of marijuana, sweat and beer. That is the first thing I became aware of. I guess I was unconscious before then. Then, another scent filled my nostrils. I can't really explain what he smelled like, but I will remember if I smell him again."

Trent leaned back in his chair. "So, the smell belonged to a person?"

"Yes. It was the scent of the first man who attacked me. The process didn't last long. He was finished in a matter of minutes. Then his partner took his turn. I counted five different men who violated me. There were others there. I think there was another girl or two there as well. I could hear her whimpers."

Trent studied Jess thoughtfully. She stated the details of the incident in such a matter of fact manner. It was as if she was relating to a friend how her day was. She was going to need a lot of therapy to get through this ordeal.

"Miss Turner, you have told me more today than you have over the course of the month."

"I feel it is time for me to move on with my life. There are still some parts that are hazy, but I am slowly remembering a lot of details."

"Will you tell me more of the last thing you remember before waking up in captivity?"

Jess nodded, "My agency was called to a location for a job at 6:00 p.m. It was a new client and I faxed over a new client package."

"Yes, we tracked that number for you." Trent interjected. "It turned out later that the number was for a copy shop."

Jess sighed. "Anyway, I arrived at the address. It was still light outside. There was a business complex at the address I gave you earlier. It wasn't the best part of town, but it wasn't the worst either.

"After I entered the office, I rang the bell on the desk since there was no one in the reception area. I think that is when I was hit on the head from behind." Jess took a deep breath and sat back in the chair.

"Thank you, Miss Turner . . ."

"Jess."

"Ok. Thank you, Jess. I know that was not an easy task."

"You have no idea. So, what progress have you made on my case? It has been over a month."

Lt. Trent leaned back in his chair. He knew that he had to arrange his next few words very carefully. He had to be honest, but he wanted her to have some hope.

"Lt. Trent, if there is one thing that I have learned as a sign language interpreter, it is how to read faces. I know that you have no leads and that you guys have hit a wall.

All I have to say is if you can't find out who did this to me, I will find out myself."

At that, Jess stormed out of Lt. Trent's office.

Chapter Three

The school Jess was to report to was Sebastian Middle School, and it was not what she expected. From the outside, it appeared to be a friendly place with its well-manicured landscape. School buses lined up in front of the school. The two police cars might have raised an eyebrow, but they sat quietly under some large, shady oak trees.

"A school this beautiful cannot be that bad," Jess thought as she parked.

The first order of business was to check in with the front office. Jess adjusted her clothes; made sure her interpreter badge was on and put on her professional attitude. This was her first assignment since her ordeal. She wanted to make sure she focused on work.

The secretary in the front greeted her pleasantly. "Welcome. Have you been to our school before?"

"No. I do not believe I have had the pleasure."

"Let me be the first to show you around. Walk with me please."

As Jess followed the young lady, she made it a point to pay attention to what was <u>not</u> being said.

"Here on the left is the lounge. You will be able to eat your lunch here. If you'd like, you can leave something in the refrigerator."

In order to enter each hallway, a card had to be scanned. Jessica noticed that the card was necessary to exit the hallways as well. One thing that Jess always advised interpreters who worked with her was to locate the exits. She located the exits, but realized that in an emergency, she would not be able to leave the building without a key card.

"Hmmm," she thought. "This doesn't seem safe."

As if reading her mind, the secretary replied, "This is a lon- term assignment. After two weeks, if you are still here, we will issue you a card so that you may enter and exit the premises. However, it must be returned at the end of your time here."

"What should I do in the meantime if an emergency happens?"

"I suggest you stay close to an adult who possesses a key card."

At that, the secretary halted in front of another locked door.

"This is your classroom. Your student's name is Michael Sanders. The teacher is Ms. Raine and the teacher's assistant in the room is Mr. Sollem."

She promptly left to return to her duties. Jess knocked gently at the door and was greeted by a string of profanity. A female voice gently scolded the children while a man, Jess guessed was Mr. Sollem, swung open the door.

"You must be the sign language interpreter. Hurry in, miss, before our runner tries to flee."

Even as he spoke, a little boy who seemed no older than 11 or 12 tried to push past her into the hallway. Mr. Sollem reached out, grabbed the young boy's arm and yanked him back into the room. The child attempted to fight the aide; however, the man was a formidable opponent. In the end, Mr. Sollem pinned the youngster to the floor, his own body on top of him.

"That is surely no way to greet our interpreter. Miss, please come in. Do not be alarmed. Sometimes our days here at Sebastian Middle School start out with a little excitement." Ms. Raine came up and shook hands with

Jess while flashing a wide grin. "Please introduce yourself to the class."

"Hello class," Jess began. She wasn't sure what to say or even who her student was. She began to sign what she was saying.

"My name is Miss Turner and I am a sign language interpreter."

"You don't have to sign to us. We can hear," chimed in one student who was sitting on top of a table.

"Oh, you must be here for Michael. He is deaf; that means he can't hear you," one student, who appeared to be the class spokesman, yelled out. "I thought you were someone interesting. He's the boy over there in the corner."

As Jess began to scan the room in search of Michael, she noticed the class was small and contained only boys. There were nine students in the class.

Michael wore a red jacket and sat with his back to the class. He appeared to be playing with some toy cars. Upon getting closer, Jess realized that he was using the cars in order to solve some math problems.

"We are in the math segment of class. Miss Turner, if you could get Michael's attention, he can be involved with our group discussion."

Jess went up to Michael and tried to move into his peripheral view. When he did not seem to register her presence, she lightly tapped him on the shoulder.

He immediately jumped up and lunged for Jess. As Jess cried out, expecting to be attacked, Mr. Sollem snatched the young boy in mid-air.

"Miss, Michael does not like to be touched." Mr. Sollem calmly guided Michael to a seat with the rest of the class while Michael eyed her uncertainly. Jess signed, *"I'm sorry"* and immediately Michael's face lit up.

"You are my interpreter? Sorry. I didn't know. Hi."

"Hi. I'm Jess." Jess gave her name sign. A name sign is a unique way of identifying individuals in sign language. *"Oh,"* he signed and showed her his sign name.

"Nice to meet you. Let's join the class and learn something new in math today."

Michael nodded and took his place at his desk.

The rest of the morning went rather well. During lunch, Jess was shown the beautiful picnic tables under some oak trees where she could eat.

"Your thirty minutes will be better spent out here in peace. Just ring the buzzer when you are ready to come back in."

Jess took this opportunity to call into the office.

"Hear Our Hands, Dylan speaking. How may I assist you today?"

"Dylan, its Jess. How are things?"

"Hi, Jess. Things here are good. Got a couple of new contracts. How is your first day back at work?"

"Interesting, to say the least. Has Lt. Trent called today?" She tried to sound casual about the question.

"No. Should I expect his call? Do you want me to patch him through when he calls?"

"No, no. That's not necessary. I was just trying to check things off my list. I will be in later this afternoon."

Jess ate her chicken salad that her mother had made for her and meditated on the events of the morning. It seemed that this school had a lot to hide. Not that it was her business, but she just had an eerie feeling.

The afternoon proved to be uneventful. As Jess packed up to leave, she patiently waited by the exit for a teacher to buzz her out. She overheard an argument in one of the small classrooms between two adults.

"That is not how it is, Amanda! You don't know all of the facts!" yelled a male voice.

"I know enough!" the female voice shrieked.

"Don't believe everything you hear!"

"I don't! I believe what I see!" With that, a pretty, young teacher came flying out of the room. She nearly knocked Jess over as she buzzed herself out of the door.

Jess took that opportunity to hurry out of the door before it locked again. But she took a moment to look back and saw Mr. Sollem come out of the same classroom. He was red in the face and he kept clenching his fists.

"Odd," Jess thought as she walked briskly to her car. "But none of my business."

Chapter Four

Back at the office, there was plenty of work for Jess to catch up on. Her agency was only a couple of years old, but she was doing well. She was not trying to be in competition with the other two big interpreting agencies. She did not take on major contracts that her small agency could not handle. Because of this, the larger agencies would sometimes send her work when they could not fill positions or if taking the contract would be a conflict of interest with other customers.

That is how she got the assignment at Sebastian Middle School. She had to make sure the file on the middle school was complete.

Also, four other interpreters desired to work for the agency. She had to process their documentation and interview them before they could begin to work.

That was just a small portion of the work left for her to do. It was almost 5 o'clock when she walked into the office. Her dedicated staff was still there, working hard.

The office manager and interpreter scheduler, Sophia Sanchez, was from New York. She moved to Atlanta to be with her family and decided she loved being a Georgia Peach. She was 28 years old, full of life, and an awesome interpreter. She kept up with the latest styles, gossip and technology. If anyone wanted to know anything about what was going on in society, Sophia had the answer. Whenever she went on a job, it was not unusual for them to call back and request her again. She brightened up every room she entered, and the Deaf community loved her.

Dylan Shumaker was a quiet, private young man. He was born and raised in Bainbridge, Georgia. Growing up as a mixed-race child in a small town in Georgia was extremely difficult and he was happy to come to Atlanta to go to school. He graduated from Georgia State University at the top of his class and realized that he did not really want a career in Telecommunications. He went back to school to become a sign language interpreter and fell in love with the language. He is also an interpreter educator, teaching others how to join the profession of interpreting.

The two of them met Jess at a silent dinner. This is a meeting between the hearing and Deaf community in a social setting, usually in a mall food court. It is called a silent dinner because the method of communication used at these social gatherings is sign language.

After their meeting at that silent dinner and hitting it off, the three decided to attend a conference together. After that, they became fast friends. In a year's time, Jess shared her vision for opening her own sign language interpreting agency. To her surprise, they were in total agreement.

"You should go for it. That's a great idea." Dylan was the first one to jump on the bandwagon.

By the end of the week, Dylan had found grants that Jess could apply for. From there emerged the "Hear Our Hands" agency.

Jess thought about this as she walked into the office. She never lost the excited feeling whenever she unlocked the door and looked around.

The first thing that caught her eye in her office was the plaque dedicated to her sister, Jazz. It read: "For my sister, who will forever be a part of me."

Jess became an interpreter for reasons totally different from Sophia and Dylan. Jess had an identical twin sister, Jazz, who was deaf. The two of them were inseparable, even creating their own form of communication.

One day, when the girls were ten years old, Jazz ran out into the street. She was chasing their cat, who had escaped from the house. She didn't notice the car flying down the residential street, and the driver was too busy to notice Jazz. The young man hit Jazz and killed her instantly.

That day, a part of Jess died also. Even though the young man was charged and imprisoned, that justice did not replace her sister and the void left in her life. However, she did not allow grief to consume her; rather, she made it drive her.

After graduating from high school, she decided to become a sign language interpreter, in honor of her sister. Going the next step and opening an agency to further serve the Deaf community just seemed like a logical thing to do.

Her co-workers were both on the phone but took time to throw her a wave. Jess went over to her desk and proceeded to bury herself in the work that needed to be done. It was about 8:30 pm before she took a breather. The front office was empty. She decided to order Chinese and work a little longer. It had been a while since she had been at her desk and she could tell. However, she enjoyed working and her food arrived quickly. She tipped the delivery person and went into the library to eat.

Jessica's favorite place in her office was the library. She loved to read, and she had filled it with many types of books. The room had plush carpet, four cozy armchairs and a faux fireplace, a heater that had the appearance of a fireplace.

Jess loved to spend time in this room and often went here to meditate. She ate her chicken fried rice and thought about her day. The students at the school were very interesting. They each had a unique set of problems and it was a challenge for the faculty and staff to address those needs. Jess had seen this type of situation before. She was very familiar with working with children with special needs. Yet, she had never dealt so closely with such severe disorders.

Well, she knew what to expect for tomorrow and she was ready. She closed the office and went home.

****

Jessica's home was a townhome in Avondale Estates, a suburb of Stone Mountain, about 20 minutes from Atlanta. She loved the area she lived in because the community took and active role in keeping it clean and safe.

Her mother was still awake when she arrived home. It was hard for Jess to get used to her mother living with her again. Louisa Turner was an intelligent woman in her 60s. She was divorced and collecting a nice alimony check. She sold makeup full-time as her work from home job. She came to live with Jess over a year ago because of her battle with breast cancer.

Jess' siblings have families so it seemed a logical solution that Ms. Louisa Turner live with her oldest daughter until she could live on her own again. Logical, at least, to everyone except Jess. She valued her privacy and was not used to another human being in the home with her. She did enjoy the company of Petey, her chocolate Labrador.

She tried not to see her mother as an intrusion, but she needed a bit longer to accept the idea completely. One major change was that Petey had to be moved outside during the day because Louisa didn't like dogs.

Jess parked in her driveway and went to let Petey come in with her through the garage. This daily ritual was much anticipated by Petey because Jess took time to clean and brush him before they went inside.

"I missed you today, Petey. You would have enjoyed the lovely area where I had lunch. The oak trees were beautiful."

They entered the kitchen to see Louisa cleaning up. The aroma of fresh blueberry muffins was still lingering in the air.

"Mama, you've been baking again." Jess ran over to hug her mother and swiped two muffins. As she bit into one, she broke off a piece and tossed it to Petey.

"I've told you about giving that mutt table food."

"But mom, Petey loves your muffins." Jess hurried out of the kitchen and up to her room. She wanted to shower and wash the day off her.

Chapter Five

The bell rang at Sebastian Middle and Ms. Raine's class began. As math was the first period of the day, Michael immediately located his toy cars and began using them to help with his multiplication skills. However, Jess could tell he was bothered about something. Time passed by uneventfully until a fellow student decided to snatch some of Michael's cars from his desk.

Michael jumped up and the two boys started fighting. Jess stepped back, unsure of what to do. When a chair flew past her head, she noticed Mr. Sollem was not there to referee. She hid next to a cabinet, hoping it would provide safety as the entire class was chanting "Fight, fight!"

Ms. Raine had already pushed the panic button on her desk and two security officers came running in. Each took a young boy and escorted him outside. Jess followed.

Surprisingly, the youngsters were not taken to the principal's office. They were taken to an area called the 'quiet' rooms. These rooms were similar to jail cells with one-way mirrors/windows. Each boy was placed in a separate 'cell' until he calmed down.

"You don't have to stick around, Miss," one officer told Jess. "We are just going to talk to him about how to behave in class."

"Thank you for the consideration, sir, but if you are going to talk to him, I need to be here to interpret."

"No, you don't!! He might have you fooled, but that boy can read lips and he understands me just fine. You go on and take a break now."

Jess hated it when hearing individuals tried to inform her how much her Deaf consumers could understand or hear. She also did not like being bullied.

She walked over to the nearest chair in front of the window and sat down. The two officers just looked at her astounded that she was defying them. They young boy in one of the cells yelled out.

"Are you going to hit us in front of that lady?"

Michael stood up in front of Jess' window and started signing.

"They treat us bad in here. Sometimes, they leave us in here all day, and we don't get any lunch. We are not allowed to use the restroom. They even . . ."

Before he could finish, the guards flipped the switch that turned on the one-way mirror. Michael could no longer see Jess and started pounding on the glass.

An officer yelled for him to stop, but Michael, who obviously could not hear the officer, continued his tantrum.

"What was he saying to you?" one officer demanded.

"He was expressing his concern about missing lunch." Jess felt bad about not telling the whole truth, but she feared the guards would take further action against Michael if she told them everything he said.

"Lunch is the last thing he will get today if I have anything to do with it."

"Now, Larry. You know it is against the law to withhold lunch from our students." A handsome, dignified officer walked up with a scolding look at the guard. He was perfectly groomed, and Jess was slightly mesmerized by his strikingly good looks.

"Ms. Turner, I do not believe we have had the pleasure of meeting. My name is Julio Chavez and I oversee security here at Sebastian Middle School. We pride ourselves in our fairness and commitment to justice."

As he spoke, he flipped the switches so that Michael and the other boy were able to see her again. Jess made a mental note of the cologne he was wearing.

Chavez continued, "I am sure these two young men have had sufficient time to think about their actions. They may return to class." At that, he left as quickly as he had appeared.

****

The 'quiet' rooms continued to bother Jess for the rest of the day. She kept thinking about what would have happened if she was not there to witness the situation.

"Ms. Raine, is Mr. Sollem sick today?" Michael's question brought Jess back to reality. She voiced to question to the teacher.

"I'm not sure." Ms. Raine turned to Jess. "The front office said he didn't even call in today. That is not like him. I hope he is not in the hospital."

Michael, who had been following the conversation, became very agitated. *"Something is wrong with Mr. Sollem."*

"How do you know?" Jess asked Michael.

"He never misses school. Find out why he is not here."

"That is not my responsibility Michael. But I will talk to Ms. Raine while you finish your science work."

That seemed to appease the youngster for the moment. He went back to his classwork. Jess went over to Ms. Raine, who shared Michael's concern.

"Michael is right. It is not like Mr. Sollem to miss any days without telling anyone."

Jess was tempted to let Ms. Raine know what she saw the other afternoon but decided against it. She was not one to gossip and didn't want to give the wrong impression.

Chapter Six

Jess was worn out. State testing had started and that meant interpreting for long periods of time. So as the children filed into the gym for P.E., she searched for the nearest faculty restroom. She needed to go all day. A coach saw her and understood her predicament. He directed her to the nearest area.

Jess had never been in this area before. The first thing that she noticed was a strong stench. She guessed that went with a bathroom in the gym. The room had two stalls, mirrors on one wall and a washer and dryer. There was a weight bench in front of the mirrors. Through another door was a shower room.

After Jess finished relieving herself, she looked around. She was naturally curious, and her curiosity had gotten her into trouble on several occasions. She wanted to find the source of that awful odor. Upon entering the shower room, she noticed that it couldn't have been cleaned in a while.

"I guess no one uses it that much."

The cobwebs were thick enough to hold a human and a layer of grime covered the floor. As Jess came out of the shower room and walked toward the washer and dryer, the stench grew stronger. It made her nauseous and she barely made it back to the toilet before she began throwing up.

"Wow! I don't know what that smell is, but it is really making me sick."

She held her nose and went back over towards the washer and dryer. She opened the washing machine lid. Inside was a dumbbell that weighed 15 pounds.

"Why would this be in here?" she wondered. She closed the lid and bent over to peer inside the dryer door. The clothes were jumbled together with a strange brown stain covering most of them. Upon looking closer, it appeared to Jess that a glove of some sort was also in the mix. Jess squatted down to get a better view and found herself eye to eye with Mr. Sollem!

Jess ran so fast out of the restroom that she didn't notice where she was going. She ran straight into Ms. Raine.

"I just saw Mr. Sollem in the dryer in the gym! We need to call the police immediately!"

****

The gym and surrounding areas were sealed off. All the faculty, staff and students were quarantined in the cafeteria. The police had to question everyone, and parents had to be called. Jess took it upon herself to call Lt. Trent because he was the only police officer she had on speed dial. She searched through the children to find Michael.

Amidst the chaos in the cafeteria, Jess saw LT. Tory Trent. Her heart gave a small leap for joy and she began to calm down. He had seen her as well and hurried over to her.

"Are you ok? I heard you were the one who found the body? Let's go find a place where we can talk in private."

"I can't. I don't want to leave Michael. He is probably worried sick right now. When will I be allowed to get back to him?"

"Don't worry. Michael is fine. Ms. Raine is keeping him with the other children until I interview you. Shall we go this way?"

Trent took Jess to the cafeteria manager's office and shut the door. He was trying to figure out where to begin.

"Lt. Trent," Jess began for him. "I have seen human beings do awful things to each other. But this is terrible. Who would want to put Mr. Sollem into the dryer? Was he dead or unconscious?"

Even as she asked the question, she knew the answer.

"Take your time and let me know exactly what happened."

After about 20 minutes, Lt. Trent had heard Jess' entire story. He wanted to pry for more information, yet, he realized that she was still fragile. Then he had an idea.

"What did you smell?"

Jess closed her eyes. "At first, it smelled like a normal gym locker room, that stale smell of sweat, urine and Lysol. Then, a different stench hit me. It was a combination of sweat, cologne and . . . and death."

"What do you remember about the cologne? If you smelled it again, would you be able to identify it?"

"I, I believe so. Yes, I think I would be able to. It smelled expensive."

****

Ms. Raine came looking for Jess so that the police officers could interview Michael. His parents had been contacted and had faxed over their consent. Michael was visibly agitated and seemed to calm down a little when Jess walked up.

"What happened? My friends are saying there is a dead body. Who is it? Is it Mr. Sollem?"

Before Jess could respond, the officer wanted to know everything the young man said. Jess told him and then set up rules for the interview. She talked and signed at the same time, something she hated doing, but for a moment she had to.

"Officer, as you ask Michael questions, please direct them to him. Then, Michael, you will respond. Please allow me time to process both the questions and answers. I

will interpret what is being said by all parties. Please be patient with me."

The officer nodded. "That sounds easy enough. Young man, why do you think something happened to Mr. Sollem?"

"He was not at school today. He never misses school and he promised to show me a multiplication trick today. He always keeps his promises. Is it Mr. Sollem? Is he dead?"

"There was a body, son. We have not released the identity yet. Any other reasons you believe it is Mr. Sollem?"

"He was upset about something yesterday." Michael's distress was evident.

"How do you know?"

"On Wednesdays, he shows us how to play chess. He didn't yesterday. That only happens when he is upset about something. And yesterday, he frowned a lot."

"Ok, Michael, is there anything else you want to tell us. Did you see anyone strange hanging around the school yesterday?"

"No." At this, Michael seemed to shut down.

****

It was well after 6 o'clock when Michael's parents came to pick him up. Jess was finally able to meet them. They thanked her profusely for staying with Michael until they could arrive.

As Jess drove home, the shock of what happened that day finally hit her. Mr. Sollem had been killed and she found the body!

She was sobbing by the time she pulled up into her garage and Petey could sense she needed him. She hugged her dog for a few minutes and just let the tears flow.

Chapter Seven

The school was closed for the rest of the week out of respect for Mr. Sollem and his family. Jess went into the office and tried to bury herself in her work. When Sophia arrived, she immediately ran up and smothered Jess with a huge hug.

"How are you? You poor thing. I saw the story of what happened on the news this morning. Why did you come in? You should have taken the day off to rest or go to therapy or something. I know you can't talk about what happened, but honey...!"

Jess smiled, extremely grateful she had friends who cared. "I know. I wanted to come in. You are going to have to be my therapist today, Sophie."

As Jess checked her email, she noticed one from Sebastian Middle School requesting an interpreter to accompany a social worker and a psychologist to Michael's home. They were doing this for all the students and realized they would need an interpreter for Michael.

"Sophia, is Dylan out on assignment today?"

"Just an early meeting this morning. He should be in in the next 20 minutes."

"O.K. I need to see him as soon as he gets in. I have another assignment for him."

The full weight of the previous day's events seemed to hit her. Jess decided to go into her library in order to try to calm down.

She hadn't realized she dozed off until she heard Dylan clear his throat in the doorway.

"Why don't you go home and rest? You have been through a lot. We can handle the office."

"I know I should. I just might later. But for now, I have a job for you. The student from Sebastian Middle School needs an interpreter at his home and I think it would be a conflict of interest for me to go. Can you handle it for me?"

"Sure, on one condition: You must take the rest of the day off. If not, we do not have a deal."

"You drive a hard bargain, Dylan. O.K., fine. Maybe I will go and get my hair done. "

As Dylan prepared to go to Michael's house, Jess called Michy at Salon Dolce' to see if she had any appointments available for the afternoon. Salon Dolce' was the equivalent of a mini vacation spa for Jess. A client could get her hair, makeup and brows done as well as schedule a massage.

Michy, the owner of the salon, had known Jess for almost 15 years. She was a tough, no nonsense stylist who transformed the trade into an art form. However, she would never sacrifice the health of someone's hair just to give them the latest styles. That fact alone brought customers to Salon Dolce' by the dozens.

The shop was painted in soft earth tones which created an ambiance of calmness. All one's senses were soothed upon entering. Soft jazz music played in the background. Scented candles were burned throughout the shop. A huge waterfall took up a large section of the waiting area wall.

Jess could feel the tension draining from her as she sat in Michy's chair. After her hair was washed and dried, Michy began to curl it. It was at this point that the tension began to return.

A client of another stylist began to talk about the murder of the previous day.

"Did you hear that they found a body in a dryer at Sebastian Middle School yesterday? I think they said it was one of the teachers."

"Girl, yes! Isn't that awful? Who would do such a thing?"

"Probably some of those wild children."

"Naw, I think it had to be another teacher."

"Well, I heard that a woman killed him because he was cheating on her with another man."

The speculations and chatter continued and Jess' stress level began to rise. Michy must have sensed it because she spoke up.

"Why don't we have a Dolce' moment and try to think positive thoughts for a few moments." She turned up the music slightly and all that could be heard were the curling irons and hair dryers.

****

As Jess pulled into her driveway, she was preparing to explain to her mother why she was home early. She hadn't told her what happened when she came home last night, and she really didn't want to talk about it now. She also wasn't sure how much she could talk about because she was bound by an interpreter's code of ethics. She had to figure out how much of the information she could share with her family.

She was spared conversation because her mother was not home when she arrived. Petey was happy to see her and followed her to her room.

When Jess was stressed, she liked to clean. She rolled up her sleeves and dove into doing her laundry, cleaning her room and vacuuming.

The hours flew by. It was nearly dusk when she heard a knock at her door. Thinking it was her mother, Jess flew down the stairs, fussing.

"Mom, have you lost another set of keys? How many times . . ." Her voice trailed off as she opened the door and was looking into the light brown eyes of Lt. Trent.

"I am so sorry. I thought you were my mother. I look a mess. I have been cleaning my house. At least it's clean. Why don't you come in?"

Jess realized she was rambling out of embarrassment and let the lieutenant in. At least her hair was done.

"Ms. Turner, I thought I would check on you after that terrible ordeal yesterday. I came by this morning and your mother told me you went in to work. I was surprised you went back so soon."

"I didn't feel like staying home. Besides, I had a lot of office work to take care of."

"I really wish you would take a couple of days off. The rest would do you some good."

"So," Jess remarked slyly, "do you want me to stay home or is that a standard department response to those who have witnessed a crime?"

Tory Trent was silent for a moment before he softly answered. "I want you to take some time off."

After finding out this information, Jess was once again embarrassed and could feel her cheeks begin to heat up.

"Please excuse my rudeness. Can I get you something to drink? My mother made some oatmeal raisin cookies. Would you like some?"

"No. I am fine. Thanks"

'That you are,' thought Jess and she slapped herself mentally. 'I've got to get my mind right.'

Lt. Trent turned toward the door. "I just wanted you to know that your help is much appreciated with this case. I know you believe we are not making any progress with your case, and you might be right. But any help you give us with this murder would be helpful. You have my number."

At that he was gone.

'What just happened,' Jess thought. 'Am I reading too much into this or did he seem like he was concerned about me? And what help do they want me to give on the case? I only found the body.'

****

Jess did not have to worry about going back to work at Sebastian for a few days. They closed the school until Wednesday of the following week. Instead of going into the office, she decided it would be in her best interest to work from home.

****

The medical examiner placed the time of death of Mr. Daniel Sollem between 2:00 – 4:00 a.m. the morning he was found. It was harder to narrow down the time because of the heat from the dryer. It was not known whether the dryer was turned on while Mr. Sollem was inside.

The police had also discovered that the address that Mr. Sollem was using as his mailing address was not his physical address. Also, his car had not been found.

Chapter Eight

Lt. Trent sat in his office with his head in his hands. He had to come up with a suspect because his boss was on his back. It seemed as if no one had any clue as to how Mr. Sollem found his way into the dryer.

A Detective Richardson rushed into his office.

"One of the teachers on the main hallway overheard Mr. Sollem and an Amanda Priest having a heated argument a couple of days before the murder. It was also reported that your Jessica Turner might have overheard the dispute as well."

"Thanks. That is just the break I needed. You can join me as I go question Ms. Priest."

"So...you are still choosing to remain without a partner?" the young detective began. But he stopped when he saw the look come over Lt. Trent's face.

"If I remember correctly, I requested your presence. Which means, I do have a partner for this assignment." Trent stormed out of his office and almost slammed the door in the face of the detective.

However, the detective was not alone in trying to discover why Lt. Tory Trent decided not to have a partner. Trent had been in the department longer than anyone and there was even an office bet as to who would finally discover the reason he worked solo.

When the detective caught up with Trent, he had already started the car and was about to drive off.

"First, we are going to stop off and see Ms. Turner. I have a few more questions to ask her. She never mentioned an argument."

When Richardson and Trent arrived at Jess' house, she had just returned from walking Petey.

"Hello guys. To what do I owe this visit? My neighbors are going to think I have been involved in illegal activities if you keep showing up at my door."

"Ms. Turner, you didn't tell us about an argument you overheard between the deceased and a woman named Amanda Priest. Why is that?" Detective Richardson jumped right into the questioning.

"Um, well, I guess it just slipped my mind. You are right! It was my first day working at Sebastian Middle School. At the end of the day, I did hear them arguing in one of the classrooms. But I did not think anything of it. When the pretty, young teacher walked out, I followed her and just happened to look back and see Mr. Sollem."

"You do realize, Ms. Turner, that you were one of the last individuals to see Mr. Sollem alive."

****

As they drove up to Amanda Priest's home, Trent had Detective Richardson double check the address.

"This is the correct address, sir. 627 Rollins Street."

"Now find the address for the victim."

"Also, 627 Rollins Street. Hmmm. Do you think they were shacking? How did we miss that?"

"We weren't paying attention and that is something we must start doing." Lt Trent parked the car and walked up the sidewalk leading to the house.

Before he stepped onto the porch, the front door swung open and a pretty, red-faced, young woman was standing before him, tissue in hand. Her eyes betrayed the fact that she had been crying for days.

"Ms. Priest."

"Yes."

"I'm Lt. Tory Trent and this is Detective Richardson. Is everything ok?"

"No! Of course not! Danny is dead! But you already know this. Isn't that why you are here? I was wondering when the police would find out. Come in."

Amanda turned and went back inside. The officers followed and she gestured for them to sit down.

I know that I should have called and confessed to you, but I just kept putting it off. I guess it would have been the right thing to do. What I did to Danny was just awful. I don't know how I am going to live with myself. However, I know I am in a lot of trouble. Should I get a lawyer?"

Chapter Nine

Lt. Trent and Detective Richardson were dumfounded. They were not sure how to proceed. It was not common for a suspect to confess to a crime so freely.

Trent started, "Why don't you start at the beginning, Ms. Priest."

"Ok. Danny and I met four years ago at a conference on Autism. We hit it off and fell in love. However, since we both work for the county, we didn't want anyone to know we were an item.

"Two years later, he asked me to marry him. We went to Las Vegas and eloped. Upon our return, we decided to continue keeping our relationship a secret. I kept my maiden name. It worked out well until I was transferred to Sebastian Middle School, the same school where Danny worked.

"The fight that we had the other day had to do with a new teacher I saw flirting with Danny. When I confronted him about the situation, he denied it. But I know what I saw. I was so mad that afternoon I could have killed him on the spot!" Ms. Priest broke down and sobbed.

Trent waited a few minutes for her to compose herself before he began to pry for more information.

"So, Ms. Priest, please continue."

"Well, that night, he didn't come home. I don't know where he spent the night. I kept calling his cell phone, but it kept going straight to voicemail. I started believing he was at that woman's house.

"I really began to worry when I did not see him at school the next day."

Detective Richardson picked up the trail. "So, tell us the events that led up to Mr. Sollem's murder."

"What?! What do you mean? I didn't kill him! He was my husband. How can you think I would do something so terrible as that?"

"You basically admitted to committing the crime," began Richardson.

"I did no such thing. I was speaking of the fact that I concealed our marriage from the police. Isn't that obstruction of justice or something?"

"Ok, Ms. Priest. We are truly sorry for your loss. We would like for you to come down to the precinct and write a report. This will help us find out what happened to your husband. I do have a couple of questions before we leave.

"Where were you Thursday morning, between 12 midnight and 5 am?"

"I was home sleep. No one was with me. Is that when my Danny was killed?" She broke down again, sobbing violently.

"Again, I am sorry for your loss. Will you allow us to look around at your husband's personal effects so that we can find clues that might lead to catching his murderer?"

"Sure. Whatever I can do to help."

****

Trent consulted his notes and realized that a cell phone was not found among Sollem's personal effects when the body was found. He wondered where his phone might be because it was not in the home either. Also, Mr. Sollem's car had yet to be discovered. It puzzled him that the wife did not come forward sooner. He believed there was more to that story. There were no laws about teachers being married to each other. So why go through the trouble to keep the relationship a secret?

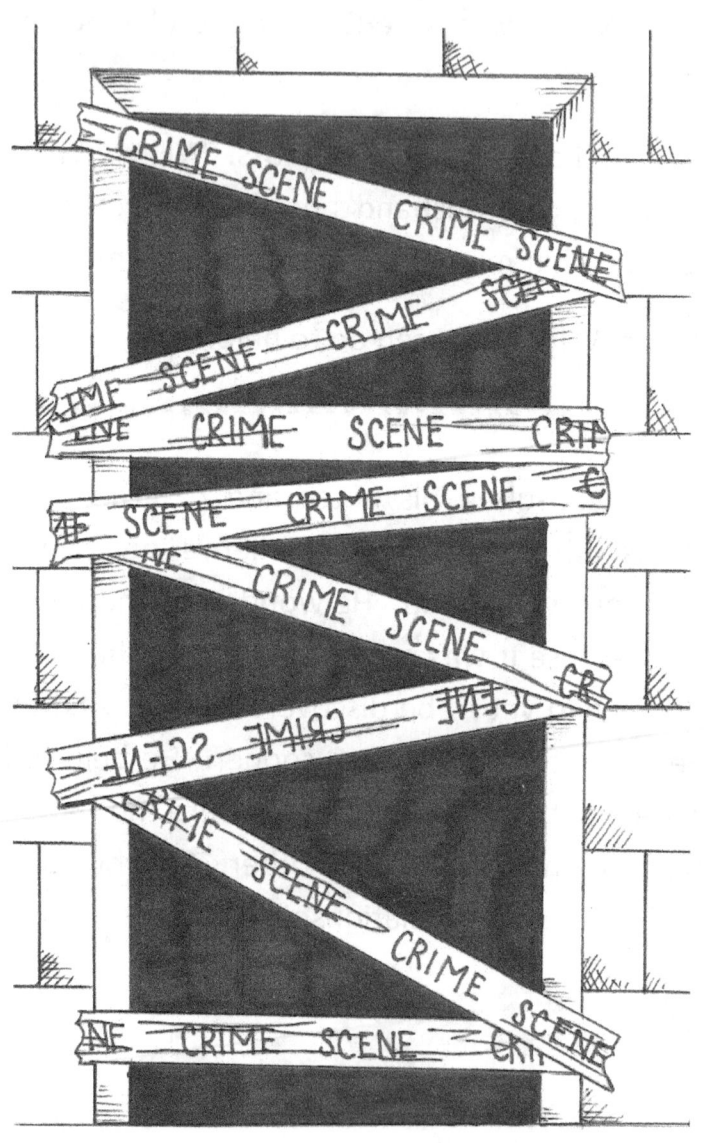

Chapter Ten

Jess woke up from her nightmare drenched in sweat. She could not stop shivering as she held and rocked herself. The focus of the dream was her gang attack, but this time she could see the face of her attacker. The face was that of Mr. Sollem! Just as he was about to attack, Jess woke up.

This had been going on for a few days. Jess had gotten to the point where she did not even want to sleep at night. However, in order to function properly, she needed her rest.

It was 4:45 am and instead of going back to sleep, Jess decided to get up and prepare for her day. However, as she began to sit up in her bed, she started feeling light-headed and dizzy. She barely made it to the bathroom before she started throwing up.

One of the downsides of working with children is that one catches every germ that children pass around. Jess figured she had picked up the latest bug and decided to load up on vitamin C. She had a lot to do and did not have time to be sick.

Today was Saturday and she was devoting this day to herself. She wanted to do some scrapbooking and watch some old movies. Petey was excited that she would be spending time with him today. She felt this when she explained to him what the plan was the day before.

Louisa was going to be spending some time with her friends on an out of town shopping trip. She was leaving at 6 am and was surprised to see Jess awake as she passed her room.

"Honey, I don't know what has been going on, but you have been acting kind of strange. Do you want to talk about anything?"

"No thanks, Mom. I just have a lot going on with work. Things should be less stressful next week."

"I hope so because you look like you are not getting enough sleep. That luggage under your eyes is something serious."

With that, Louisa left to enjoy her day out.

✱✱✱

Three hours and two movies later, Jess and Petey decided to go out for a walk. Jess collected Petey's leash, her water bottle, treats for Petey and some doggy doo bags. After that, the two set off.

The Fall time, when the leaves began to change and the air became cooler, was Jess' favorite time of the year. The crisp, cool air did a world of good for both Petey and

Jess' spirits. The two of them took turns singing (and howling) different songs.

One section of the neighborhood was being repaved, so Jess and Petey took a detour to an area that led outside of their community. Being that it was such a nice day, the two of them continued walking until the neighborhood started to change. They stumbled upon a section of neighborhood where graffiti was colorfully spray painted on the side of buildings.

Jess took time to study the graceful flow of the lettering. Graffiti always mesmerized Jess, even though it defaced public property. As Petey pulled her along to the next segment of building, Jess' heart froze in her chest. There was a loud roaring in her ears as she stared, mouth agape.

The symbol on the wall in front of her was the same symbol that was on the wrists of the men who raped her!

****

When Jess regained her composure from the shock she experienced, she dialed Lt Trent. She knew it was a Saturday and it was possible he was not in. Yet, she had to try.

Her heart sank when his voicemail came on. She pulled herself together and left a message.

"Lt, I am sorry for bothering you. I think I might have found a clue to my case. Please call me back as soon as possible."

After she hung up, Jess snapped a picture of the image so she could show it to the police later. She did not know if she would be able to make it back home. But Petey, sensing her mood change, started leading her towards home. She made sure to note the intersection so that she could let Lt Trent know when he called back.

She hoped she didn't have to wait long.

****

Trent rarely overslept. Yet this beautiful morning, not only did his alarm not go off, his internal clock did not either. He had been working so many hours that his body seemed to send him into hibernation.

He awakened refreshed, but also feeling as if something was not quite right. He checked his phone and realized, to his chagrin that he forgot to forward his work phone to his cell phone.

He called the office phone and was waiting for his message to come on so he could punch in his code. As soon as he heard Jess' voice, he sat up straight in his bed.

Even as he was dialing Jess' number, he was jumping into his clothes. Thankfully, he had taken a shower the night before.

"Hello." The anxiety was still oozing from Jess' voice.

"Jess, are you okay? Where are you? What do you mean you found a clue?"

"I'm home now. I was out walking Petey and we came across some graffiti that I recognized. I took a picture of it. Do you want me to send it to you?" Weariness clouded Jess' tone.

"I am on my way to you. Are you ok?"

"Yes, Petey and I will wait for you to get here."

When Trent arrived at Jess' home, she was still in a daze. She invited him in and went into the study.

A large bay window opened overlooked the back yard. The study was a nice, cozy area with several books, 2 easy chairs and a small table. Petey was laying at Jess' feet and he seemed equally troubled.

Jess was looking out of the window and seemed as if she were miles away.

"OK Jess, start at the beginning."

She began to tell him how she took a detour because of the construction in her neighborhood. She explained about the graffiti on the buildings at the intersection of Grater Road and Berry Street.

Then she took out her phone and showed him the picture.

"I saw this same symbol on the inside left wrist of at least two of my attackers. I remember it clearly, even though a lot is hazy. I believe I was drugged or something."

"What makes you say that?" Trent was curious because she had never mentioned that before. He wanted more details.

"I know I had a headache because I was hit on my head, but I felt drugged. It was as if my entire body was made of lead. I know that could not have just come from me being hit.

"Lt, I have a question for you. I haven't even asked this since the ordeal. How did I get to the hospital?"

Trent was wondering when she would get around to asking that question. Her unconscious body was found with two others in the middle of the warehouse where Jess had been summoned. An anonymous phone call was made from the pay phone at FedEx Kinkos.

After learning this information, Jess remained quiet. Then she spoke.

"It seems as if someone wanted us to be found. How are the other women?"

"All that I can tell you is that all of you are coping in your own way. I cannot tell you much more than that."

"I knew I heard someone crying. Can the picture of the tattoo help in finding who did this to us?"

"I hope so, Ms. Turner. I hope so."

Chapter Eleven

The OCs were notorious throughout Atlanta for causing mayhem of all sorts. The gang was especially known for being violent for fun. They would randomly pick on a person walking around the wrong neighborhood at night and end up sending them to the hospital.

The OCs were also the main supporters of the prostitution ring that plagued downtown Atlanta. The hookers reported to the pimps, the pimps reported to the gang members and paid a percentage of the earnings to them. If the money was not right or paid in a timely fashion, a pimp could be put out of business – permanently.

They were not a group to be trifled with and it was with great resignation that Trent recognized the graffiti as belonging to them. Each member, when initiated, had a certain emblem tattooed on the inside of their left wrist. That is exactly where Jess said she noticed the design. If the OCs were responsible for the attack, it was going to be very hard to convict them.

The Gang Task Force had been trying to infiltrate the OCs for years. Whenever an undercover officer was successfully recruited, it was only a matter of a week or two before his identity was discovered. The OCs would brutally kill the cop. The same would happen when female officers tried to go undercover as girlfriends or hookers. The only difference was that the female officers would be raped and murdered.

Trent secretly suspected that the OCs had an informant inside the department. He never voiced this to anyone else because he did not know who he should trust. Now, Jess' investigation would lead to him having to at least talk to someone in the Gang Task Force. He would have to give them as little information as possible in order not to put Jess in further danger.

****

As Trent was filling out paperwork, Jess was enjoying her Sunday afternoon hanging out with her best friend, Tami West. Tami was married and had two children. She worked as a receptionist at a dental office.

Jess and Petey drove the 20 minutes to Tami's. When Tami opened the front door, she immediately knew all was not well.

"Jess darling! I told you that you went back to work too soon. You look awful. Have you been sleeping?"

Jess loved her friend's candor and as she embraced Tami, she began to cry. She felt as if the weight of the whole world was suddenly on her shoulder and she could not stop crying.

Tami just let her release. She was not aware of all the details, but she knew that something was terribly wrong. She knew enough about her friend to know that Jess would let her know what was wrong when she was ready.

****

The children were playing with Petey as Tami and Jess were washing dishes in the kitchen.

"Jess, you don't have to talk to me, but I can see that you need to talk to someone about your attack. You don't look well, and your mom told me you are having nightmares."

"Tami, you know me so well. But I have been dealing. True, I'm not sleeping. But I need to tell you something. Don't ask me questions. I will tell you what I can."

Tami knew that Jess' job required that she keep a lot of information confidential. Naturally, she was surprised to hear that Jess was about to share.

"Tami, I stumbled across a dead body. I can't get the man's eyes and smell out of my head. I haven't told mom because she will ask a bunch of questions that I cannot answer."

Tami just listened and waited for her friend to continue. She secretly cursed herself for not having any hot chocolate. She knew that hot cocoa always brought Jess comfort.

"I can't get his face out of my head. Maybe I should go to therapy. I just don't like doctors."

"It is a necessary evil, Jess. Maybe the talking will do you some good."

"There's more. While walking Petey yesterday, I saw some graffiti. The picture was the same as the tattoo on my attackers' wrists. I almost passed out. That's why I called Tory."

"WHO?!"

"Oh, Lt. Tory Trent. He is the police officer handling my case."

"Ok. You need to back up. You called him by his first name. And don't tell me that you can't tell me because it's confidential!"

"There's nothing to tell. I told him to call me Jess and he wants me to call him Tory. Nothing more." But even as she was speaking, she could not help but to start grinning.

"Jess, this is your last warning. You had better spill it. Tell me more!"

"Ok, ok." And Jess began to talk.

****

On the ride home, Jess realized she felt better. She also felt a little bold. She decided to call Trent on the premise of talking about her case.

"Tory Trent," he announced on the first ring.

"Hi, this is Jess. Jess Turner. I hope I am not bothering you."

"Of course not. I was actually sitting here doing some research about the tattoo."

"Any leads?"

"Well, not really, but I would like to discuss something with you."

"I'm in the car now. Do you want me to come inside the precinct?"

"No. I have a better idea. I have not eaten dinner. I was going to go to the Diner on Ponce. Want to meet me there?"

"Sure. I need to drop Petey off at home first. Then I will meet you there. Text me the address please."

Not only did she need to drop Petey off, she needed to change her clothes and make herself presentable enough to eat with Trent.

She tried not to be overly excited as she ran into the house. Lt. Trent was not asking her out on a date. He was just going to discuss the case. He could have done that over the phone. But he chose to invite her out with him.

"Don't think too much about it, Jess," she told herself. "This is just business."

****

Half an hour later, Trent was inside the Diner on Ponce, wondering why he did not just have Jess show up at the precinct.

"I wanted her to be comfortable as we talked about the situation." His attempt at self-talk failed.

"Who am I kidding? I think I like Jess and I want to know her better. But now is not the time."

As he was sipping his water, Jess walked in. She looked stunning in a simple pair of jeans and a Yankees shirt. Simple, yet beautiful.

"Sorry it took me so long. Hope you didn't wait to order." Jess slid into the booth across from Trent, hoping she sounded casual. The truth was she was extremely nervous.

"No problem. My waitress, Tina, has been keeping me company." He grinned and his dimples exploded on his cheeks.

"I waited because I was not sure if you had eaten or not."

"I had dinner already at my best friend's house. But I would love some hot chocolate."

Trent ordered his meal and a hot chocolate for Jess. "While we are waiting for our meal, why don't I tell you a few things? The insignia belongs to the gang called the OCs. They are a violently, notorious gang."

"Yes, I have heard of them. Haven't they killed every police officer whom you guys have sent in undercover?"

"That is correct. Jess, I am going to tell you a secret. I believe someone inside the department keeps the OCs abreast of our activity. I am trying to handle your case myself, so as not to put you in anymore danger."

Jess thought for a moment before she spoke. She appreciated Trent telling her this information.

"I have already been in danger. My life will never be the same. I am appreciative that you are using discretion in this matter. Thank you."

The perky, young waitress, Tina, chose that moment to bring her hot chocolate. She placed it in front of Jess, all the while gazing at Trent.

"Do you need anything else, honey, before I bring out your meal?" She made sure she bent over low as she whispered to Trent.

"No ma'am. I am good. I have everything I need." As he said this, he turned to Jess. The full power of his dimpled grin was directed to her. "And you are very welcome, Jess."

The waitress, seeing that her use of her feminine wiles was going unappreciated, rolled her eyes and walked away.

"So, Trent, where do you plan to start on this investigation?" She sipped her cocoa slowly, allowing its warmth to overtake her.

"I want to check some gang chatter to see if there is any word about the attack. Members usually like to brag about things like this.

"Let's talk about something else. You certainly look a lot better than you did yesterday. Did you enjoy spending time with your best friend?   Tell me about her." Trent hoped that this question would open the way to learn more about Jess.

****

They spent the next hour talking and laughing. Jess learned that Trent was an only child and his mother lived in Red Bank, NJ. His father died when he was 11. He had never been married, though he was engaged twice.

"So, Jess, have you ever contemplated jumping the broom?"

"I've thought about it. Just haven't found the one yet. I know my biological clock is ticking, but marriage is not anything I want to rush into."

Tina came and threw the check on the table.

Trent chuckled. "Tina was a lot nicer before you arrived. I think she is a little jealous. Let's get out of here before she starts throwing dishes. By the way, your cocoa is on me."

"Why thank you, officer." Jess gathered her purse and the two of them left.

Trent walked Jess to her car. "Please drive home safely. I will call and check on you tomorrow."

Chapter Twelve

Early Monday morning, Amanda Priest received a phone call from Ron's Auto Body.

"Miss, uh, I guess Priest." The voice on the phone had a thick Southern accent.

"Yes."

"This is Johnny from Ron's Auto Body. Mr. Daniel Sollem brought his car here a week ago and he hasn't come to pick it up yet. We have been calling his cell phone, but it goes straight to voicemail."

"Wait. Yes, I do remember that he was going to drop his car off to get his brakes fixed. OK. Someone will be by there to pick it up shortly."

Amanda immediately got into her car and drove to the police precinct. She ran in. "I need to speak to Lt. Trent."

A receptionist showed her to Lt. Trent's office. He stood up behind his desk as Ms. Priest rushed in.

"I know where my husband's car is!"

"O.K. Where?"

"Ron's Auto Body. It's about a mile from the school. He took his car in Monday night to get his brakes fixed. I was supposed to drive him home but forgot about it after the argument.

"It totally escaped my mind when he didn't show up that night. Then he was found dead a couple of days later.

"It wasn't until I received a phone call this morning that I remembered."

"Well, Ms. Priest. We appreciate you coming in. Please fill out the appropriate paperwork so that we can pick up the car."

As Amanda Priest left, Detective Richardson popped his head into Trent's office. "Some people have all the fun. It seems like there is always a pretty, young woman coming out of your office."

"Get ready to roll out. We are about to go to Ron's Auto Body. Sollem's car is there. I am hoping to find out who killed him from something in his car."

When they pulled up to Ron's Auto Body, Johnny greeted them.

"Can I help you?"

"We are here to pick up Daniel Sollem's car. Here is the appropriate paperwork." Richard handed him the documentation.

"Has anyone been in Sollem's car? Has anything been taken out of the car?" Trent was already putting on gloves.

"Well, the guys drove it when they fixed the brakes and did a test drive. But that was a week ago."

As Trent examined the car, he opened the glove compartment. As he emptied it, he found a cell phone. He immediately bagged it and called for another officer to take it to the lab.

"Have them call me as soon as they can verify that it belongs to Sollem."

Further examination brought up nothing out of the ordinary. But it did leave several questions. Who picked up Sollem from the repair shop? Did he attempt to walk? Did the person who gave him a ride also kill him?

****

As Trent was in his office looking over the evidence from the car, he could not help feeling that the widow knew more than she was telling him.

He picked up the phone to call her. At that same moment, his cell phone started ringing. It was Amanda Priest.

"Lt. Trent, I have a confession to make. I have not been entirely truthful with you and your department. I wasn't honest about our argument and it is bothering me.

"You see, Danny thought that someone at work was getting a little friendly with me. I guess that's why the fight escalated to the point that it did. I wanted to tell you this now, before you found out yourself."

Trent was puzzled. "What exactly are you trying to tell me, Ms. Priest?"

"When you look at all of our phone records and everything, you might see that I have been communicating with a friend of mine and I don't want you to think he had anything to do with it."

"After we do our investigation, we will be the judge of that. Please give me the name of your friend."

"I really don't understand why you need to know his name. There is nothing going on between us. And I know he had nothing to do with Danny's murder."

"Ms. Priest, that is for us to investigate, not you." Trent was losing his patience. "Either you tell me his name, or I will charge you with obstruction of justice!"

Amanda sighed, reluctant to continue. "Well, since you put it like that, his name is Julio Chavez."

"Isn't he head of security at Sebastian Middle School?" Trent asked as he shuffled through a file.

"Yes, and we are good friends, nothing more. Danny had a problem with that. I knew our friendship would come out as you checked phone records.

"Ms. Priest, I don't like you. I don't like the fact that your husband was killed, yet you continue to mislead police. I still do not believe you are telling me everything now. But I promise you this: I will get to the bottom of this!"

At that, Lt Trent hung up.

Chapter Thirteen

Julio Chavez was surprised when Richardson and Trent showed up at his apartment.

"Detectives! I was not expecting to see you again anytime soon. What can I do for you?"

Detective Richardson made a move towards the door. "May we come in?"

"How long do you guys plan on staying? I am on the way out."

"We don't need to come in. We just figured that the questions we need to ask you are kind of sensitive. You might not want to talk about these things in the hallway of your apartment building." Trent proceeded to open his little black book.

"Are you and Amanda Priest having an affair?" Trent asked loudly.

"What?! Wait. Come in."

As the trio walked deeper into the apartment, Chavez was becoming uneasy.

"Now, what is this about an affair?" Chavez did not offer the police officers a seat.

Trent turned toward Detective Richardson and waited for him to continue the questioning.

"Right, um, Mr. Chavez, were you having an affair with Ms. Amanda Priest?"

"First of all, we are both consenting, single adults. If we were having an affair, we would not be doing anything wrong. But to answer your question, no, there is nothing going on between Ms. Priest and myself."

"That's not the story we were told by Ms. Priest." Detective Richardson was on a roll.

"She must have been reading more into our working relationship. As head of security, it is my responsibility to ensure the safety of all faculty, staff and students. I pride myself on doing a good job."

"What does that entail?" Trent interjected.

"In the case of a female teacher, if she is working late, after dark, I or one of my men will walk her to her car. Maybe she misread my motives."

Trent was not satisfied with the answer. "Why would she misread your motives? She was already married."

Chavez looked surprised. "What! She never said she was married. You know what. I don't like what you officers have been insinuating. Since I am on my way out, you can kindly take your leave as well."

****

The administration at Sebastian Middle tried to make the return to school as smooth a transition as possible for the students and staff. The principal requested a meeting with Jess first thing in the morning to ensure that she was ok.

As soon as Jess left the principal's office and made her way to Ms. Raine's class, Michael came running to her, his hands flying.

"Slow down, Michael. What's wrong?"

"I have a lot to tell you but first I want to meet the new teacher. He looks mean. I don't think Mr. Sollem would like him. Do you think he plays chess?"

At this moment, Ms. Raine rushed over to Jess and gave her a big hug. "Ms. Turner, we are so happy you returned. We thought you might not after what happened. Let me introduce you to Mr. Jackson."

Mr. Jackson, the replacement for Mr. Sollem, was transferred from another school within the county. He was a big, burly, black man who no nonsense demeanor terrified the children, including Michael.

Michael grabbed her hand and led her to Mr. Jackson as Ms. Raine followed. He surprised everyone by breaking out into a big smile. "You must be the sign language interpreter. I was hoping you would come so I could talk to Michael."

As he was talking, Jess was interpreting. But before she could formally introduce him, he stopped her. Then he began to sign.

"Hello. My name is Leroy Jackson."

Everyone was stunned. Michael was the first to move. He jumped up and down and signed, *"He knows sign language! He knows sign language!"*

"Ms. Turner, do not fear. I only know a little bit of sign language. Your job is safe. I used to date a girl whose brother was deaf."

Michael was undeterred. *"Do you know how to play chess? Mr. Sollem used to teach us on Wednesdays before he died. Did you know Mr. Sollem? Do you know that someone killed him here at the school?"*

"One question at a time, son. Yes, I play chess. No, I did not know Mr. Sollem, but I know he would want you to get your education. So why don't we see what Ms. Raine has to teach us today."

The rest of the day was uneventful for Jess. The students had no difficulty falling back into their routine. However, Jess did notice that Michael was somewhat preoccupied despite Mr. Jackson's best efforts at trying to make him feel comfortable.

The next morning, Jess arrived a little earlier in order to discuss with Ms. Raine the agenda for the day. As they were wrapping up, Michael burst into the room, his face red with excitement.

"I just saw the pretty teacher arguing with another man. Do you think he is going to die too?"

"What?!" Jess was asking before she caught herself.

"What is he saying?" asked Ms. Raine.

Jess relayed the information. Ms. Raine quickly shut the door so no other students could come in. She then took a seat beside Michael.

"Michael, dear. What are you trying to tell us? Start from the beginning and take your time." Ms. Raine tried to appear calm. Yet, she was visibly concerned. However, her anxiety was clear on her face.

"I saw the pretty teacher arguing with Mr. Sollem before he died. Now I see the pretty teacher arguing with the security man. Maybe he is going to die also. Maybe the pretty teacher killed him. She looks very mad."

Turning towards Jess, Michael asked, "Can we call your friend, the policeman? He seems nice and he could try to protect all of us."

Jess was totally at a loss as to what to do. She did not want to get further involved. Instead, she wanted to get as far away as possible. But secretly, she wanted to call Lt. Trent as well. She slowly felt as if her control was slipping away.

Ms. Raine interrupted her thoughts. "Maybe we can talk to the principal. Michael might be on to something. Do you think your friend could find time to come by?"

"I honestly have no idea. This is uncharted territory for me. If the principal says it's ok, maybe he should call."

"Ok. We will see what he says."

As Ms. Raine called the principal, Michael wanted to know what was going on. Jess filled him in just as the other students were starting to file in with Mr. Jackson.

When Lt. Trent received the phone call from the principal at Sebastian Middle, he was happy for the diversion. Throughout the years, he had found it helpful to walk away from a troubling aspect of a case and work on something else. Later, he would return with a fresh eye.

The situation with Julio Chavez had him stumped. He could not put his finger on it, but he knew that there was more to the story than he was telling the police.

On his drive to the middle school, Trent wondered if he would see Jess Turner. He could not figure out why just the thought of her name brought a smile to his face. He did not have the time or the patience for a relationship. Yet, this did not stop him from wanting to get to know her better.

The assistant principal greeted Lt. Trent at the door of the school. He had a stack of papers in his hand.

"All of the students here have a signed document from their parents giving them the permission to talk to you. So please feel free to speak to any student. We took this measure as a precaution. I am glad we did."

"Thank you. I appreciate you doing that. It makes my job easier. If you could show me to the student, Michael Sanders, I would like to go on and take his statement."

The assistant principal showed him to the conference room where Michael was sitting with Ms. Raine and Ms. Turner. The child did not look at all afraid. Rather, he looked pleased with himself.

"Good morning, ladies. Good morning, Michael." Trent remembered to turn and speak to Michael as if he could hear.

The adults barely had a chance to respond before Michael started excitedly signing.

"The pretty teacher is the one killing people. When she has a fight with someone, they die." He then acted as if someone cut his throat, he stuck out his tongue, rolled his eyes to the back of his head and fell to the floor.

Everyone was stunned.

Finally, Michael opened one eye to see if his audience was still watching. He next opened the other eye and started grinning.

Lt. Trent was the first to recover. "Michael, why don't you get up and tell us what you saw?"

Reluctantly, Michael sat in his chair. *"Today, I saw the pretty teacher arguing with the security man. I could not hear what they were fighting about because I am deaf."* Michael chuckled.

"This is the same teacher that argued with Mr. Sollem before he died. So maybe she is going to kill the security man too."

Lt. Trent tried to suppress a slight smile. The young man was eager to assist in solving the mystery. He might be of some help.

"Michael, what else did you see?"

"The security man kept shaking his head and backing up. Finally, he just turned and walked away from her. She was still mad. Her face was very red."

"O.K. Michael, you have been a big help. If I need your help again, can we talk?"

"Yes. You're cool. I like helping the police."

After Trent talked to Michael, he asked him to sit outside while he talked to Jess. Ms. Raine had to return to class.

"Did you talk to him at all about what you saw earlier between Ms. Priest and Mr. Sollem?"

"No sir. Of course not."

"O.K. Sorry. I had to ask. I just needed to make sure that the information was not tainted. How have you been, Jess?"

"As well as can be expected. How about you?"

"I'm doing fairly well. I have been very busy with this case. If you think of anything else, just give me a call."

****

Trent decided that he would speak to both Priest and Chavez while he was still at the school. He went to the main office and was informed that he had to wait for Ms. Priest to take her class to P.E. before he could interview her.

The secretary called Chavez up to the office while Trent waited in the lobby.

Chavez was not happy to see Trent. "So now you are starting to harass me on my job. What can I do to make this stop?"

"Just continue to answer my questions, and truthfully, and this will be over before you know it."

"Well, come to my office. That way we can talk privately." Chavez led Trent down a long, narrow hallway that led to the security office.

As Trent entered the security office, he was immediately struck by the coldness of the office. Not just the temperature but, the room felt so impersonal. No photos or pictures lined the concrete walls and a musty odor seemed to permeate the air. The only light came from a window tucked away in the corner and a ragged, dusty curtain placed over it.

Trent cut to the chase. "What did you and Amanda Priest argue about this morning?"

"What?!"

"You were seen having a heated discussion this morning with Ms. Priest. What about?"

"Who saw us? I demand to know who has been spying on me!" Chavez walked over to the window and pushed back the curtain.

"That is not the point. Are you going to tell me what you were fighting about?"

"It is none of your business. What is more, I am going to file an official complaint. I should not have to be harassed in this manner. I am also an officer of the law. I was expecting a little more courtesy from you."

"That's funny. I was always taught that you have to give respect to get respect. You have given my department a hard time since we started this investigation."

Chavez paced to the window that overlooked the outer office. "You are right. I apologize. I have been completely rattled since this murder happened here, at my school, on my watch. I know you are doing our job. I want to help wrap this up as well.

"I suppose that is why I confronted Ms. Priest this morning. I was hoping she would tell me something that would help me solve the case."

"Mr. Chavez, you don't have to solve the case. That is my responsibility. I can appreciate your willingness to help. But don't go and get yourself in trouble trying to question people. Leave that to me.

"There is something you can help me with. I see the other security officers watching monitors. However, when I asked for the tapes, I was told that there are none."

"Lt, we do not record what happens here. That is basically for a protection. Sometimes, the tactics that are used to control a situation are less than desirable. It is safer not to be on record disciplining the children."

"Are you and the staff here doing anything illegal?" Trent was understandably troubled.

"Of course not. Just controversial. Parents are encouraged to come to the school at any time and observe how their child is being treated."

"And just to review, no one sitting at the monitors saw anything suspicious the day the body was discovered?"

"No. The area where the body was found is the faculty and staff area. Cameras are not placed in those designated areas. But that is not common knowledge."

"So whoever killed Mr. Sollem knew that there were not any cameras in that area."

Trent meditated on that fact for a while. Chavez stayed quiet, evidently having considered this possibility already.

"Well, Chavez, thank you for your time. I may need to speak with you again later. Please feel free to contact me if you come up with anything you believe will assist in this case." Trent handed Chavez his card.

"I will definitely do so. Would you like me to show you out?"

"No, I think I can manage. Thanks."

Lt. Trent now had more information about the case than he had previously. While walking towards the front, he saw Jess Turner outside eating her lunch under the oak trees.

She looked very peaceful, munching on her sandwich while she checked her emails on her phone. The sunlight fell upon her face in such a way that her face had a glow. The piles of multicolored leaves at her feet seemed as if they formed plush carpeting.

A smile lit up Jess' face as she saw Lt. Trent approach her. "If I had known you were staying for lunch, I would have saved you some. Did you find out anything new?"

Trent smiled. "I might have. I figure that if I stay around here long enough, someone will eventually confess."

Upon seeing Jess' puzzled look, Trent began to tell her about the conversation with Chavez.

"So that must mean that whoever killed Mr. Sollem knew exactly where the cameras were. I guess that does make it an inside job. That's kind of scary." Jess began to shiver a little and drew her jacket close to her chin.

"It appears that way. I think I will stick around and do a little more investigating."

Trent got up to leave and stopped short. "Can I call you this evening? Maybe we can get a bite to eat or something?"

Jess grinned. "I would love that."

****

As Jess and Lt. Trent were chatting outside, Chavez was watching them from the window in his office.

"So that is his source of information. That snitch!!"

****

After Trent lunched with Jess, he went in search of Amanda Priest. She was in her classroom, grading papers and seemed surprised to see Lt. Trent.

"Well, hello Lt. Have you come with new information? Do you know who killed my Danny?"

"Not yet, I'm afraid. But I do have a few leads. I was surprised to see you back at work so soon. Didn't you want to take some time off?"

"No. I do better by keeping busy. I have a good support group here. But if you do not have any new information, why are you here?"

"It was reported that you had a heated discussion this morning. Do you care to share what it was about?"

"Huh. I mean, who told you I had a 'heated discussion'? Why would anyone call you? What's going on?"

"Ms. Priest, it is a simple question. What was your argument about?"

"I did not have an argument with anyone. I might have been upset, which is understandable, I just lost my husband."

"It seems to me that individuals would feel more inclined to comfort you than argue with you."

"I was not arguing with Julio!" As soon as she said it, Amanda Priest realized the mistake she made.

"That's funny, Ms. Priest. I never said who this alleged argument was with. Thank you for confirming that you and Mr. Chavez did have an altercation."

"I would like you to leave now. If you want to question me again, you will have to do so in the presence of my attorney. Goodbye Lieutenant!"

✳✳

As Trent was driving back to the precinct, he was forming a picture in his mind as to what happened. He needed to be sure before he arrested anyone, but he began to feel that he was very close.

When he walked into his office, he began piecing together his bits of information. Trent had been compiling data for almost an hour when Richardson walked in.

"Guess what!"

"Don't want to guess. Just tell me."

Richardson was grinning like he had just won the lottery. "Chavez called Sollem the night he went to drop his car off for repairs. Funny he didn't mention that. The call lasted a minute and a half. That's a little too long to be leaving a message."

"So, Chavez might have been the last person to talk to Sollem that night. That is lining up with my theory. Thanks."

Chapter Fourteen

Michael stayed after school for a tutoring session. Naturally, Jess had to stay with him to interpret. So, she was ecstatic when 6 o'clock rolled around. Exhausted, she searched for the nearest restroom. For obvious reasons, she avoided using the restroom in the gym at all costs, even when it was the closest one.

She decided to use the one in the teacher's lounge. It was usually very clean and afterwards, she would be able to get a snack from the vending machine.

As expected, the hallways were deserted as she made her way to the lounge. Most of the faculty and staff had gone home for the day.

While in the restroom, Jess was mentally reviewing what she needed to do when she went into her office, when she heard a noise. It sounded like a door opening.

"That's funny. I didn't see anyone else around here," she thought to herself.

Upon exiting the restroom, Jess did not see anyone. So, she went to the vending machine. She was so intent on making her choice she did not notice the figure come up behind her.

Then everything went black.

****

Lt. Trent was feeling good. He had a gut feeling he was on the right track. Julio Chavez had to be the murderer. Now, all he needed to do was collect proof and build his timeline. The motive was simple: Amanda Priest and Julio Chavez were having an affair. Of this, Trent was sure. He had been comparing phone records as well as time logs when employees left the school. It was obvious that the two of them spent a lot of time together.

However, Trent could not figure out why Chavez would need to kill Sollem. Maybe there was no reason that made sense. Chavez was a murderer and Trent had to stop him.

****

Jess had a headache. She wasn't sure why. She was lying in her bed with a throbbing pain in the back of her head. For some reason, she wasn't comfortable either. It felt like her bed was made of stone.

She began to focus and realized she was not in her bed at all. She was on the cold floor of some sort of dark cell. The memory of getting hit on the head was coming back to her. Did this mean she was still at the school?

93

She began to feel around the floor and the walls just so she could gather information about her surroundings. Yes, she strongly believed she was still at the school, in one of the 'quiet' rooms. She knew there was a one-way mirror and it was set so that she could not see outside.

"Who could have done this to me? And why?" She tried to find a way out of the room.

Upon exploration of the room, she discovered that her purse had been taken.

"So, no cell phone," Jess thought with disgust. Even so, she was not even sure she would get reception in the bowels of the school.

"There has to be a way to let someone know where I am." Not having success finding a way to escape, she sat down in a corner to figure out how she could open the door.

She needed her purse. In it she had a plethora of items to assist her in her dilemma.

****

Suddenly, Trent realized that something was not right. The only problem was he did not know what. He decided to call Jess and see if she had the same feeling. He liked the idea of bouncing things off her. Their 'date' was set for later that evening, but he could not wait.

He called her phone and it went straight to voicemail.

"Hmmm. Maybe she stopped by her office," he thought. He decided to call.

"Hear Our Hands, Sophia speaking."

"Hi Sophia. This is Lt. Tory Trent. I was calling for Jess, er, Ms. Turner. Is she available?"

"Oh, hi Lt. Dreamy!! She was supposed to show up an hour ago, but we haven't heard from her. Have you tried her cell phone?"

"Yes, but it's going straight to voicemail."

"That's strange. Recently, the only time her phone goes straight to voicemail is when she is at the school she has been working at."

"Thank you, Sophia. If she checks in, please let her know I called."

"I will."

****

Trent began to know what that feeling of dread was about. Something was wrong with Jess and he thought it had to do with the Sollem case.

Sophia had mentioned that the only time Jess' phone went straight to voicemail was when she was at Sebastian Middle School. Suppose she was still there?

He decided to drive by the school to check things out. On the way to the school, he took a route that led him past Jess' house.

He stopped to see if she if she happened to be at home for some reason. As he walked up sidewalk, leading to the door, Louise Turner opened it abruptly.

"Please tell me you know where she is."

"I'm sorry, Mrs. Turner, I don't know where she is."

"She is not answering her phone. Since her ordeal, she is always sure she to contact me or at least answer my calls. I have been trying for hours."

"Mrs. Turner, I have an idea where she might be. I will check it out. I will call you when I find her. Write your number down and take my card. If you hear anything before, I call you, call me."

After exchanging numbers, Trent went back to the car and headed for Sebastian Middle School.

****

Jess tried to gather her wits in the darkness. There had to be something that she could do to get out. After her search, she realized that there was no knob on the door. She would have to find another way to get out.

She had lost it for a moment and yelled until she was hoarse. Jess knew that no one could hear her, but she could not give up hope.

Her only consolation was that she was supposed to go to dinner with Tory Trent tonight. Hopefully, he would suspect something was wrong when she didn't answer his call.

She knew her mom was probably worrying as well. But she could not dwell on that. She needed to find a way out. And while she was thinking about that, she needed to find out *who* put her in there.

Jess remembered that Trent had hinted that the murderer probably worked at the school and was familiar with the placement of the security cameras.

"Concentrate, Jess. You have got to remember something," Jess talked to herself out loud.

"Wait a minute. What I smelled today, I have smelled before, that day when they put Michael in the 'quiet' room. Yes, that chief security guy. That's right! I'm sure of it!"

"But that is not the same scent I smelled in the gym where I found Mr. Sollem. Maybe there is more than one murderer."

Jess was trying not to get hysterical with her thoughts. Now that she suspected Mr. Chavez of throwing her in the quiet room, she tried to figure out why.

"Why me? Because I found the body? But I never pointed the finger at him or anybody else?"

****

While Jess was in the 'quiet' room trying to sort out information, Julio Chavez was pacing in the security office. He acted on impulse when he grabbed that interpreter. Now he had to figure out what to do with her.

He did not necessarily want to kill her because he was not sure of how much she knew. Yet, he did not want to take the chance that she did know something.

His office phone rang.

"Julio. I was wondering if you were still at work. Why don't you come over? We could order some Chinese food," Amanda Priest was pleading. "I'm feeling kind of lonely."

"I'm not sure it is a good idea tonight. I have a lot of work to do here."

"I could bring you dinner. That way you could still get your work done."

Chavez gave in. "OK, OK. Come on to the school. Just ring the buzzer at the front and I will let you in."

Chapter Fifteen

Lt. Tory Trent pulled into the parking lot at Sebastian Middle School and cut off his car lights. As he drove in, he noticed two cars. One of the vehicles looked like it belonged to Jess. He pulled up his computer and ran the license plate through the system.

The vehicle did belong to Jess! He ran the tag on the other car, and it came back registered to Julio Chavez.

So, his hunches proved right on both accounts. He immediately called for backup. He also called Detective Richardson's cell and informed him to get a warrant and come to the school.

While he waited, Trent tried to figure out why Chavez would want Jess. She had not said anything to implicate him.

"Wait a minute. The security office window overlooks the area where we had lunch today. Maybe Chavez saw us talking together and suspected her of being the one who told about the argument. That would be a good reason to snatch her." Trent was eager to get out of the car to start searching for Jess.

While he was sitting in the car, another vehicle arrived in the parking lot.

****

Amanda Priest rolled up into Sebastian Middle School with a smile on her face. Julio had not spent time with her since the death of her husband and she was lonely. So, if it meant hanging out with him while he was at work, that was fine.

She parked next to Julio's car. She noticed there were two other cars, besides Julio's, in the lot. So maybe the whole crew was working late. She didn't bring food for everyone.

She was so busy trying to figure out how to explain her presence to the other security officers, she was oblivious to Lt. Trent approaching behind her.

****

"Richardson, how close are you?"

"I am around the corner."

"Amanda Priest just pulled up and I see a way to get in the building unannounced. I will try to leave a way in for you, but if I can't, do what you need to do."

Trent quietly got out of the car and watched as Ms. Priest gathered up the Chinese food bags. She seemed lost in thought and did not notice as Trent slipped up behind her.

"Don't be alarmed, Ms. Priest. This is Lt. Trent. Please turn around slowly."

"Uh, um, hi, Lt. Trent. What are you doing here?" Amanda Priest was clearly uneasy.

"I could ask you the same thing."

"I was bringing dinner for the security guys. Nothing more."

"Well, I don't want to keep them from their dinner. Why don't we go in together? The catch is that you will not let on that I am with you. Are we clear?"

"Yes sir." They walked up to the front door of Sebastian Middle School. Amanda Priest pressed the buzzer and looked up at the security camera.

"Julio, it's me."

The door clicked open.

****

Chavez did not know what to do. He was sure of one thing. He could not tell Amanda what he had done. He had a good thing going and didn't want to ruin it. Soon, he would marry Amanda and have access to her money. He did not want to do anything to jeopardize that now.

He had just checked on Jess and noticed that she had given up trying to find a way out. Soon he would give her a tranquilizer and transport her off the campus. But first things first; dinner with Amanda.

He buzzed her in when he heard the doorbell. He didn't bother to really look at the camera. He began to tidy up the office to ensure that nothing would give away his secret.

****

On the way to the security office, Lt. Trent had his gun drawn. He didn't know what to expect and he was not sure how much Ms. Priest was involved.

"Do you mind telling me what is going on? Why is your gun out? I demand an explanation."

"Ms. Priest, you are not in any position to demand anything. Just keep quiet and stay behind me."

The two of them silently walked down the dark hallways. When they came upon the security office, Trent was the first to open the door just a crack. He wanted to see what he was walking in to.

It appeared that Chavez was the only one in the room. So, tonight was a date.

He walked in the room and ordered Chavez to "FREEZE". Chavez turned around and reached for his gun.

"If you do that, you will be making a huge mistake. I'm in the mood to shoot you, so don't make me do it."

Chavez froze and looked between Amanda Priest and Lt. Trent. "What is going on? Amanda? Did you call the police?"

"No. He just..."

"Quiet. I will do the talking. Julio Chavez, where is Jess Turner?"

"How should I know? You are the one who was all cozy with her earlier today. You tell me."

"I will give you one more opportunity to answer my question. Where is Jess Turner?"

"I told you I do not know."

****

Detective Richardson and the other officers quietly entered the building. Lt. Trent left the door propped open. They walked through the building, looking in classrooms, searching for Jess.

Lt. Trent had briefed them on the situation. He had the sneaking suspicion that Jess was locked up in one of the 'quiet' rooms.

The team already had a layout of the school from the investigation. It was easy to find the 'quiet' rooms.

****

Jess had given up hope. She would have to stay here until someone found her. She was exhausted and frustrated. The stench in the room was overwhelming.

She started feeling lightheaded. At the same time, she thought she heard footsteps. Terrified, Jess tried to stand up, a little too quickly, and passed out.

****

Trent was still holding the gun on Julio Chavez when Detective Richardson carried an unconscious Jess into the room.

"Is she ok? Why isn't she moving?" The desperation was apparent in Trent's voice.

"She is just unconscious. There is a nasty bump on her head, but I have called EMS." Richardson laid Jess gently on a table.

One of the other officers arrested Chavez and read him his rights. Trent was torn between running to Jess and questioning Amanda Priest. The latter won out.

"Ms. Priest, please sit down and tell me what you know about what is going on tonight."

"I promise you that I do not know what is going on." Amanda broke down into tears.

At that moment, EMS rushed into the room and started attending to Jess.

"Richardson, take Ms. Priest down to the precinct for questioning. I am going to ride along with Ms. Turner to the hospital."

Chapter Sixteen

Jess blinked. She had terrible headache and she felt very weak. She knew she was in a hospital room and knew exactly what had sent her there. What she did not know was who was sitting in the room with her.

"Look who is awake. How are you coping?" Lt. Trent's dimpled smile came into focus.

"So, you found me? Have you called my mother?"

"Yes, she is out there getting us some coffee. She has been here the whole time.

"We arrested Julio Chavez and we have Amanda Priest for questioning. Do you feel up to tell me what happened?"

"There is not much to tell. I came out of the restroom, went over to the vending machine and got hit on the head. My head still hurts."

"Yes. Your doctor says you have a concussion. You will have to take it easy for the next couple of days."

"I am about to go to the precinct and try to close this case. I will come and see you as soon as I am finished."

Lt. Trent leaned over and kissed the top of her forehead. "I was so worried about you this evening. When I return, we need to talk."

At that, he was gone.

****

Back at the precinct, Julio Chavez and Amanda Priest were ready to talk.

"Yes, Julio and I were having an affair, but I never told him to kill my husband. I did not even know he did. Why would he do that? I loved my Danny!" Ms. Priest once again began sobbing.

Detective Richardson was not convinced. "Did Mr. Sollem know about the two of you? Do you think he might have threatened Mr. Chavez?"

"No, not Danny. He would have told me. We were striving for honesty in our relationship. Well, I mean, I was honest about everything except the affair."

"Ms. Priest, we are going to have to hold you for more questioning. I'll be right back."

Richardson was prepping to question Chavez when Lt. Trent came running into the office.

"What do you have? Fill me in."

"Will do. How is Ms. Turner?"

"She is ok. She has a concussion, but she will be ok. I need details now!"

Detective Richardson filled him in as they walked to the interrogation room that held Julio Chavez.

Lt. Trent cut to the chase immediately after walking into the room.

"Why did you kill Daniel Sollem?"

"I know the drill. I am tired of fighting it. I killed him because he was going to go to the media about our use of the 'quiet' room."

"It had nothing to do with the affair you were having with his wife?"

"No. She was going to leave him anyway. Why do you think she did not change her name when she got married?

"It is against the law to continue use of the 'quiet' rooms, and that goodie-two-shoes was going to blow the whistle. That would have ruined my career."

"Did Ms. Priest have anything to do with this?"

"She is beautiful and everything, but she is not the smartest girl out there. She had no clue. I think she would have stopped seeing me if she knew."

"Explain to us what happened in detail."

"I picked up Sollem from the car repair shop and drove him back to the school. He had already let me know that he wanted to turn me in. I pretended that I was going to put them out of use.

"When we went into the school, I told him that I had tools in the gym, I picked up a weight and hit him over the head when he wasn't looking. Then I stuffed his body into the dryer."

"And all of this is because you did not want to discontinue use of the 'quiet' rooms." Lt. Trent could not understand.

"Yes. I do not expect you to understand. I would not have been able to get a job anywhere. The principal was not aware that the rooms were still in use. But these kids are delinquents. We have to use whatever means necessary."

Detective Richardson had more questions. "Why did you kidnap Ms. Turner?"

"She was such a snitch. She was always sticking her nose where it did not belong. I had to deal with her."

"What exactly were your plans for her? Were you going to kill her?"

"I'm tired of talking. Get me a lawyer."

Chapter Seventeen

Jess awakened to the familiar sounds of a hospital room. She slowly became aware of an IV in her arm and a throbbing pain in her head.

Then, she heard his voice. Lt. Trent was talking to someone. Was someone else in the room? Wait, no, he was talking on the phone.

"Richardson, I hear what you are saying, but I just don't buy it. You mean to tell me that Chavez killed Sollem because he was about to report him to the authorities concerning those rooms he was using. That does not make sense. There must be more, and I believe the wife is involved as well.

"Do some more digging. We can't close this case yet."

As Tory Trent hung up his phone, he turned and noticed Jess.

"You are awake! How are you feeling?"

"As well as can be expected, I suppose. Did you catch Chavez?"

"Yes, and he confessed."

"But you don't believe him. Talk to me. Tell me why."

"I could be wrong. Don't worry yourself about it. You just concentrate on getting better."

"Tory Trent, I have been laying in this bed for who knows how long. I need something to get my mind off my situation. Spill it!"

Lt. Trent chuckled. "Yes ma'am." He grabbed a chair and moved closer to Jess' bed.

"Let's keep this information between us. I can't share everything, but I will let you know what I can.

"Chavez says that he killed Sollem because he was going to inform the powers that be of his use of those rooms in the school. He claims that he killed Sollem to silence him and that he grabbed you because you were too nosy about those rooms."

"You mean the 'quiet' rooms, right?" When Trent nodded, Jess continued. "That's not true." Jess tried to sit up in her bed.

"I know. But I must be able to prove it. . . Wait a minute. How do you know it is not true?"

"I told you before that I do research. I <u>am</u> nosy. When I first saw the 'quiet' rooms in use, I started digging."

Jess grimaced in pain. Immediately, Lt. Trent jumped up to assist.

"You ok? What can I do?"

"Nothing. I'm good. I just needed to adjust and didn't realized how sore I was."

"Maybe I should call the nurse."

"No. Now pay attention. The State of Georgia is already aware that the 'quiet' rooms are still in use at Sebastian Middle School. The county was given an ultimatum – 'Stop using them or funding will be cut.' They have until the end of the school year to comply.

"So, that cannot be the motive for killing Sollem."

"There must be another reason. Hmmm...That is what I thought." Trent paused, turned and smiled at Jess. "You know, we make a good team. I just have to find a way for you to stay out of trouble."

****

Armed with the new information from Jess, Lt. Trent was whistling as he left the hospital.

He pulled out his phone and called Detective Richardson.

"My hunch is proving correct. The authorities are already aware of the use of those rooms. So that couldn't be the motive.

"Let's check the financials of Sollem, Chavez and Priest. Something has to pop."

"Will do, boss. How is the patient doing? Is she going to be ok?"

"Yes, she seemed in good spirits."

"That's good. I will get the information you requested right away."

****

Lt. Trent's phone rang.

"Hello."

"Good evening, you are getting a call from a Video Relay Center. A person who is Deaf or Hard of Hearing is calling you. His name is Michael Sanders." The operator on the other end of the phone sounded tired.

"Ok. What does Michael want?" thought Trent.

"*Hello police officer Trent. This is Michael, from Sebastian Middle School. I want to know if you have caught the person who killed Mr. Sollem.*"

"As a matter of fact, Michael, we have."

"*I knew you would catch him. Now we can feel safe at school. Thank you.*"

"No problem. That is my job. Now go to bed and stop worrying about things."

After that, the phone line went dead. Trent had never received a call from a relay service. It was an experience. Yet, he had a feeling that he would be receiving more calls of that nature if he associated with Jess Turner.

Also, he considered whether he had told the young man the whole truth. Had he caught all the murderers?

Chapter Eighteen

"We missed something major!" Detective Richardson was excited as he rushed into Lt. Trent's office.

"I have singlehandedly located the missing piece of the puzzle."

Trent smiled. He decided to let Richardson gloat in his triumph for a moment.

"Lay it on me."

"Well, we had previously studied the financials of the three individuals you had requested. Nothing seemed out of the ordinary. But there was another important document that none of us thought to examine."

"Well, Richardson, are you going to tell me or keep standing there grinning?"

"There was a will. Both of Daniel Sollem's parents died. They were very wealthy. Daniel Sollem has a brother named Justin, who is currently incarcerated.

"In the will left by the family, it states that whichever son marries and remains so for at least two years will inherit the family fortune!"

Trent slowly digested what Richardson was telling him.

"Amanda Priest and Julio Chavez have been running around together. The marriage between Priest and Sollem, although real, was really a scam. Both Priest and Chavez were after Sollem's money.

"So when Sollem dies, his money is all left to Priest, who splits it with Chavez." Trent was starting to feel the excitement along with Richardson.

"But we are still missing one piece. I don't think the will was common knowledge. So how did Priest and Chavez find out about it?"

"That is a good question. We can't really arrest them until we figure that part out. We need to make sure that our case is airtight this time, or they may get off on a technicality." Trent stood up, grabbed his coat and rushed out of the door.

****

When Jess woke up, the sun was shining through the dozens of flowers on the windowsill. The aroma of the roses, Jess' favorite flower, filled the room. The sweet perfume soothed Jess for a moment.

Then she remembered where she was.

"Hey, you are finally back with us. How are you?" Tami had been sitting with Jess all night.

"I feel ok. You are definitely a sight for sore eyes." Jess adjusted herself as Tami leaned in for a hug.

"Where's mom?"

"You know that staying in hospitals is very difficult for, you know, dealing with the cancer and all."

"Yeah. You are right. I wasn't thinking."

"She had been here for hours before she left."

The hospital phone rang. Tami answered.

"Well, it seems that you have a visitor on his way up to see you. I might just finally get to meet this mystery man." Tami was straightening Jess' hair and fluffing her pillows.

"He is on his way now?!"

"Yes, I think he called from the car, so it will be a minute. We need to get you looking presentable. Do you want to change your nightgown?"

Jess once again was grateful to have a best friend as wonderful as Tami. She did not even have to speak, and Tami knew what to do.

"No, just give me the robe that I asked you to bring. It is bright and colorful and will not make me look so sick."

As Tami searched for the garment, she continued. "Lt. Tory Trent sounds very nice. He was very concerned about how you were healing. He also wanted to know if you were up to helping him with a question about the case."

Jess avoided looking at Tami because she did not want to answer any questions she might have about Trent right now.

Tami continued her work of making Jess look presentable. Using a warm bath cloth, she cleaned Jess' face and neck.

"Will you stop fussing over me like I am a child? I can still do some things myself!"

"If you saw how you looked before I worked my magic, you would be very thankful now. O.K. I'm finished. You can quit whining now."

Tami finished up just in time, because at that precise moment, Lt. Trent walked into the room, carrying a dozen red, pink and yellow roses.

He smiled his deep, dimpled grin. "Well good morning. How are you today? And you too nurse. Why, the nurses are getting prettier and prettier in this hospital."

Tami blushed as she introduced herself. "I'm Tami, Jess' friend. It is a pleasure to meet you."

"The pleasure is all mine, Ms. Tami."

"O.k. Enough already. Quit with the mushy introductions and let's get to work. What did you have to ask me about the case?"

"Oh, I see the patient is grumpy today. Did she not sleep well?"

"I was here all night. She slept well enough. Maybe she is hungry. I haven't seen her breakfast. Let me see if I can go and locate it. Will you be alright with her in here for a moment?"

"I will try my best."

With that, Tami breezed out of the room, adding a little extra sashay to her hips.

"You should feel privileged to have a friend like that. She seems like a real gem."

"She is. I love her dearly. I just hate to keep her from her family. She has two great children."

"You should be out of here soon."

"I hope so. By the way, thank you for the beautiful flowers. I love them."

"I called your mother and she told me roses were your favorite. I wasn't sure what color to buy, so I chose three. I see everyone else bought you roses too."

"A girl can never have enough roses. Yours are perfect."

A deep pause settled over the two of them. Jess began to get uneasy. Trent must have felt it too, because they began to talk at the same time.

"You have. . ."

"How are you . . ."

Like a gentleman, Trent bowed and asked Jess to go first.

"Ok. Trent...I mean Tory, you had some questions about the case you wanted to ask me.

"Yes. I wanted to bounce a few ideas off you and see what you came up with. But only if you are feeling up to it."

"Go ahead. I don't know how much time you have before Tami gets back, so give it to me.

"Well, these are general questions, so I will be able to continue talking about them when your friend returns."

"Good, because I am here now. What did I miss?" Tami placed a tray in front of Jess. It contained grits, scrambled eggs, and dry toast.

"If I were a woman and I wanted to find out about a man's money, where would I start?"

Jess and Tami looked at each other and started giggling.

"What? Let me in on the joke."

"If you want to know about how much money a man does or does not have, you don't ask him. You need to start with others who know him. People love to talk about other people's money." Jess was starting to forget she was in a hospital bed.

Tami chimed in. "If you ask him, he is going to lie. He will lie to impress you or lie to keep you from liking him for his money."

"Ladies, in this case, there is a will. The will stipulates that certain things need to happen before the money is released. I don't see this as information that would be readily accessible to neighbors and coworkers."

"You could also check with jealous ex-girlfriends. They are always a good source."

"I don't think either that source would work. You see, the parties who found out about the money were strangers. The only living relative he has is in prison."

Tami's eyes lit up. "People tend to spill their guts in an anonymous group. If the guy has a brother in prison, he might be a member of a family of prisoner's support group.

"While in these meetings, he might just talk about his money, and people might start to look really hard into who he is."

Jess looked over at her friend with admiration in her eyes. Jess and Tami had different upbringings. Jess would never have known about a family of prisoner's support group.

"Thank you, ladies. You have given me a lot to mull over. I appreciate your help." With that, Lt. Trent grabbed Tami's hand and kissed it gently. As Tami was blushing, he leaned over and kissed Jess on the forehead.

Before Jess could respond, Lt. Trent was gone.

Chapter Nineteen

Armed with the new information from Jess and Tami, Trent was whistling as he left the hospital. He pulled out his phone and called Detective Richardson.

"My hunch is proving correct. The authorities are already aware of the use of those 'quiet' rooms. So that could not possibly be the motive for the murder."

****

The Atlanta chapter of Support for Families of Prisoners (SFP) met every other Wednesday evening at 8:00 p.m. at a library in Dunwoody.

Trent decided to arrive twenty minutes early in the hopes of talking to whoever was in charge. He had chosen to wear a pair of jeans with his favorite black Harley Davidson boots. He wanted to look less like a cop, so he topped the look off with a black shirt and a thick, black leather jacket.

As he entered the library, he followed the signs that led to a room in the back. A cheerful woman was bustling around, whistling while she put the chairs in a circle.

"Well, hello there. I'm Tina, the moderator. You're new and you are early. You can give me a hand and help me set up. The others will be here soon."

"No problem. I actually came early to ask a few questions."

"What are you, a cop?" The lady turned to get a good look at Trent. "Well, yes you are. I could tell the moment I looked at you."

"Yes ma'am. If I show you some pictures, will you be able to tell me if the individuals are members of this group?"

"I'm not really supposed to, but being that you ae cute and all, I guess I could. I just love a man with dimples."

Trent showed her pictures of Priest, Sollem, Chavez and a few others just to mix it up.

"I have only been the moderator for this group for a year and a half. Another moderator and I split the schedule for these classes. I have never seen these individuals."

Disappointed, Trent placed the pictures back in his jacket pocket.

"However, Janie has been coming here for 15 years. If they have ever been here, she would know them.

"But I don't want you to spook the group. Would you mind waiting until after the meeting to ask her? Come back in an hour and a half."

Trent occupied the next hour looking through magazines in the library. He was lost in thought, ogling the pictures of fancy cars. His cop senses did not kick in to alert him that someone was standing behind him.

"Are you a cop?" The raspy voice of a decades long smoker interrupted his thoughts. "Never mind, I know you are. I'm Janie. What do you want to ask me?"

"Well, hello Janie. I am Lt. Tory Trent. I would like to know if you know any of these individuals from the group."

As Trent showed Janie the pictures, he watched her eyes for any signs of recognition. When she came to Sollem's picture, she smiled.

"I remember this one. Has a brother in jail. Story was sad because he lost both his rich parents too. I guess he came here to find a sense of belonging."

"Did he connect with anyone specifically?"

"No, not that I can remember. I do know that there was one girl that would always ask him questions about his inheritance. She would do that during group.

"One day, the guy in the picture told her that it was none of her business and did not want to discuss it anymore."

"Do you remember what this young lady's name was or how she looked? "

"Don't know her name. She was a redhead with bright, green eyes and a full face. But something about her seemed. . ."

"Seemed what?" prompted Trent.

"Well, artificial. She was almost too perfect. I don't know. Maybe I didn't trust her because she would always sit somewhat apart from the group, in the shadows, sort of.

"But after your friend told her to mind her own business, she did not come back."

"Well, Ms. Janie, here is my card. Please call me if you can think of anything else. It has been a pleasure."

****

"I know that if I can find that one missing piece, I can solve this case. Maybe it is here. What am I missing?"

Lt. Trent was in the squad room pacing back and forth in front of a magnetic whiteboard which held all the photos and paperwork pertaining to the case. Among the data was a copy of the will left by Danny Sollem's parents. In it was the stipulation that the son who married and remained so for two years would inherit a vast sum of money as well as the family estate. The other son would be left nothing.

Detective Richardson saw Lt. Trent pacing and gave him his distance. He knew that to disturb him while he was lost in thought would unleash the beast. He decided to follow up on a lead on his own. Richardson grabbed his keys, preparing to drive out to Phillips State Prison, in Buford, Georgia.

****

Justin Sollem was serving a 15-year sentence for armed robbery. This was ironic because his family was wealthy. If they were alive, he did not want for anything. He was spoiled as a youth and turned to committing crimes for fun. This was his second time in prison.

When he walked into the visitors' room at Phillips State Prison, he was surprised to see a police officer, a detective.

"Do I know you?"

"Not yet. I'm Detective Richardson with the APD. I have come to tell you about your brother."

"I was wondering when someone would find out about me. I saw what happened on the news. It sure would have been nice to go to his funeral." There was no sadness in Justin Sollem's eyes for his brother.

"I am sorry for your loss. Did you know anyone who would want to murder your brother?"

"Besides me? Just kidding. Nope. He seemed so happy with his new wife. The two of them seemed made for each other, like Ken and Barbie."

"Do you think his wife would have killed him?"

"Why should she? Since she was married to Danny, the money would all be hers soon. But I wouldn't really know what was happening on the outside, would I?"

Richardson chose to ignore his sarcasm. "If you think of anything that will help us solve your brother's murder, call me."

"No sweat. I have nothing else to do in here. Oh yeah. You might want to talk to that one guy who came to visit me a few years ago."

"What guy and why should I talk to him?"

"He was asking a lot of questions about my parents and their will. It was after they died. He said he wasn't a lawyer, but a cop of some kind."

"Did you get a name?"

"I don't remember, but you are a detective..."

"What specifically did he want to know?"

"He asked if something happened to Danny after he received the inheritance, who would get his money and the estate."

"And what did you time him?"

"Danny's wife would get everything. I wouldn't get a dime!"

****

The pieces were all starting to fall into place. Lt. Trent was very proud that Richardson had taken the initiative and visited the prison. Even though it seemed small, that visit cleared up a lot of the questions in Trent's head.

Chapter Twenty

"I have told my lawyer that I do not wish to speak with you anymore." Julio Chavez defiantly informed Lt. Trent at the police precinct.

"I am aware of that. But as your lawyer is also aware, we have found some more evidence in this case. I can prove that your story about why you killed Sollem is not true."

"I need a moment to talk to my client." Chavez's lawyer was dressed in a very expensive suit. His shoes alone cost more than Trent made in a month.

"Take your time. Your client will have plenty where he is going."

As the lawyer whispered to his client, Trent sat back and meditated on how he was going to present the evidence he had discovered to them. He did not want to show all his cards, but he wanted to let them know he meant business.

"My client is willing to give up an accomplice if you are willing to charge him with a lesser crime."

"Excuse me. I do not believe you guys are the ones who called this meeting. I called it. That means I get to tell you what I want. I want you to be put away for life, you and your accomplice.

"I want you to make retribution to the families you hurt in the process and return any money that you have swindled in the past.

"So no, I am not going to charge you with a lesser crime!" Trent was so angry his head was starting to pound. He could not believe that Chavez wanted to make a deal.

The lawyer whispered something in Chavez's ear. Chavez sighed but started to speak.

"Amanda and I have been working together for the past 10 years. We find different ways to swindle unsuspecting people out of their money. So, when we stumbled upon Sollem, we decided to con him. All we had to do is get Amanda to stay married to him for two years.

"All was going well until he found out about the scam and was going to draw up papers to divorce Amanda after he received the money.

"We had worked too long and hard on this project, so I tried to shut him up. He was not aware of my involvement at the time, so it was easy to get him to come back to the school with me.

"The rest is history."

"No, Mr. Chavez. Your career as a con artist is history."

Chapter Twenty-One

Amanda left for the lawyer's office in a hurry. She had to find a way to speed up the release of the inheritance money. There was a nice, stiff breeze outside and this aided her in her disguise.

She had on an all-black, swing dress, black tights and some modest, black patent leather pumps. The wind tugged lightly at the scarf she had tied around her head. Her big sunglasses were opaque enough to barely see her eyes. To an outsider, she really did look like a widow in mourning.

She smiled to herself as she thought about some of her other disguises. Her favorite one was when she was a red head and attended Support for Families of Prisoners meetings. However, today, she decided to let her natural blond hair flow.

As she waited at the elevator, she tried to work up some convincing tears. The uniform would do no good if she could not do her acting part.

As she stepped out onto Simpson and Shark's plush carpet, Shark's secretary greeted her pleasantly.

"Good morning, Ms. Priest. Mr. Shark is expecting you. Please go right in."

Amanda glided through the door that was being held open for her. Larry Shark had done well for himself. He spared no expense when it came to decorating his office. The sofa and love seat alone cost more than most people make in a year. The handmade desk was imported from overseas; the art that decorated the walls was the envy of the most avid collector.

Shark had been Amanda's attorney for a decade. He never asked questions and for this he charged a hefty price. He knew the law, as well as how to get around it at times. This quality is what Amanda was looking for today.

"Ms. Priest. How nice to see you again. I hope that all is well. You sounded upset on the phone. What can I help you with?"

As Amanda took a seat directly across from the desk, she tried to conjure up a few tears. "My husband recently was murdered. As you know, according to his parents' will, he was supposed to inherit money after being married two years.

"He was murdered the week of our two-year anniversary. So how do I go about getting the money from the inheritance?"

"I am so sorry for your loss. I do have a copy of the document and have reviewed it. Let me go and retrieve it now."

As Shark left the room, Amanda Priest got up to look out of the huge window that overlooked the city. The view from the 21st floor was intoxicating. She was so enamored by downtown Atlanta that she did not notice Shark come back in the room. But he was not alone.

The voice of Lt. Trent intruded on her thoughts. "Amanda Priest, you are under arrest for the murder of Daniel Sollem and also for felony fraud."

Amanda turned around swiftly; all traces of the grieving widow vanished from her face. "You do not know what you are doing. You idiots do not have the facts. The person you should be charging is Julio Chavez. This whole thing was his idea."

"Ma'am, we already have Mr. Chavez in custody, and he has explained the entire con to us. I have eyewitnesses who can identify you and we have also been talking to Daniel Sollem's brother in jail. I am no lawyer, but you have a lot of evidence stacked up against you."

As Detective Richardson cuffed Priest, she turned and spoke to Larry Shark. "So, what happens to the money now?"

"Well, Ms. Priest, there is a clause in the will that stipulates that if one brother were to die before the money was awarded, the surviving brother has to follow the same criteria in order to inherit the money. Were both brothers to die before inheriting, the money would go to specified charities.

"If you had done a little more research, you would have known this. I will give you the names of some excellent criminal attorneys. Perhaps one of them can assist you in your predicament."

****

Tory Trent finished typing up his report on the Daniel Sollem case. As he was gathering his belongings to go home, he decided to call Jess.

"Hello."

"Hi Jess. This is Tory Trent. I wanted to let you know that we closed the case on Daniel Sollem today. We arrested Amanda Priest as well."

"I knew there was someone else involved. I smelled another scent in that room. Wow. She killed her own husband."

"I will give you details later. Get your rest and get out of that hospital." Trent smiled. Just a few months earlier, he had not even known Jess Turner. Now he was thinking about her every day.

EPILOGUE

Tami walked into the hospital room with a bag of fresh clothes for Jess. If there was one thing she could say about Jess, it was that she was like the Energizer bunny; she just kept going and going. She was already talking about going back to work.

Jess was sitting up eating breakfast when Tami walked in. Her face lit up as she laid eyes on her best friend.

"Jess, there are other ways of getting us to spend more time together. You don't have to go get kidnapped and knocked in the head. I would have come to visit you more often."

"Well, you know me. Did you bring my clothes? I am so ready to get out of here!"

"Yes, I have your things. Come on; eat up so we can go. Hospitals give me the creeps."

As Jess changed her clothes, Tami gathered up her belongings and packed them for her. She was worried about her friend. She never liked to talk about things, but always found a way to get involved in stuff. The drive to Jess' house was going to be used to get to the bottom of Jess' feelings.

"I know you are over there wondering if I am ok. I am. And no, we are not going to talk on the way home."

"I really hate when you do that. You always seem to know what I am thinking. Well, have it your way. You are going to have to talk to me one day."

At that moment, the doctor walked into the room.

"Jess, I see you are ready to be discharged. I have instructed the nurses to get the paperwork for you to sign so that you can go home.

"You will need lots of rest and I want you to take the next couple of days off from work to help you recuperate.

"However, there is one more thing we need to talk about."

"Yes, doctor. What is it?"

"Do you want to talk privately?" He asked as he looked at Tami.

"No, she can stay. Is something wrong?"

"Well, I got the results back from all the blood tests that we ran. And, well, there is no easy way to say this..."

"Just spill it," Tami was getting nervous.

"Well, the pregnancy test came back positive. You are going to be a Mother."

The next in the series:

Followed by:

DOUBLE

BEGINNINGS